CONJUROR'S
HOUSE

OTHER WILDSIDE LIBRARY CLASSICS

Quality Street, by J. M. Barrie

The Free Press, by Hillaire Belloc

Seven Keys to Baldpate, by Earl Derr Biggers

The Malakand Field Force, by Winston S. Churchill

Armadale, by Wilkie Collins

My Lady's Money, by Wilkie Collins

The Black Douglas, by S. R. Crockett

The Viaticum and Other Stories, by Guy de Maupassant

The Safety Curtain and Other Stories, by Ethel M. Dell

The Mormon Prophet, by Lily Dougall

The Forty-Five Guardsmen, by Alexandre Dumas

Tales of Allan Quatermain, by H. Rider Haggard

Stories of Ships and the Sea, by Jack London

From Out the Vasty Deep, by Marie Belloc Lowndes

The Quickening, by Francis Lynde

If I Were King, by Justin Huntley McCarthy

Jimgrim and the Woman Ayisha, by Talbot Mundy

The Jester of St. Anthony's, by Arthur Stanwood Pier

The Queen of Spades, by Alexander Sergeievitch Pushkin

Boyhood, by Leo Tolstoy

Marjorie at Seacote, by Carolyn Wells

From the Valley of the Missing, by Grace Miller White

A House of Pomegranates, by Oscar Wilde

The Canterville Ghost, by Oscar Wilde

The Picture of Dorian Gray, by Oscar Wilde

See www.wildsidepress.com for additional titles.

CONJUROR'S HOUSE

A Romance of the Free Forest

STEWART EDWARD WHITE

WILDSIDE PRESS

CONJUROR'S HOUSE

Published in 2006 by Wildside Press, LLC.
www.wildsidepress.com

CHAPTER ONE

The girl stood on a bank above a river flowing north. At her back crouched a dozen clean whitewashed buildings. Before her in interminable journey, day after day, league on league into remoteness, stretched the stern Northern wilderness, untrodden save by the trappers, the Indians, and the beasts. Close about the little settlement crept the balsams and spruce, the birch and poplar, behind which lurked vast dreary muskegs, a chaos of bowlder-splits, the forest. The girl had known nothing different for many years. Once a summer the sailing ship from England felt its frozen way through the Hudson Straits, down the Hudson Bay, to drop anchor in the mighty River of the Moose. Once a summer a six-fathom canoe manned by a dozen paddles struggled down the waters of the broken Abítibi. Once a year a little band of red-sashed *voyageurs* forced their exhausted sledge-dogs across the ice from some unseen wilderness trail. That was all.

Before her eyes the seasons changed, all grim, but one by the very pathos of brevity sad. In the brief luxuriant summer came the Indians to trade their pelts, came the keepers of the winter posts to rest, came the ship from England bringing the articles of use or ornament she had ordered a full year before. Within a short time all were gone, into the wilderness, into the great unknown world. The snow fell; the river and the bay froze. Strange men from the North glided silently to the Factor's door, bearing the meat and pelts of the seal. Bitter iron cold shackled the northland, the abode of desolation. Armies of caribou drifted by, ghostly under the aurora, moose, lordly and scornful, stalked majestically along the shore; wolves howled invisible, or trotted dog-like in organized packs along the river banks. Day and night the ice artillery thundered. Night and day the fireplaces roared defiance to a frost they could not subdue, while the people of desolation crouched beneath the tyranny of winter.

Then the upheaval of spring with the ice-jams and terrors, the Moose roaring by untamable, the torrents rising, rising foot by foot to the very dooryard of her father's house. Strange spirits were abroad at night, howling, shrieking, cracking and groaning in voices of ice and flood. Her Indian nurse told her of them all—of Maunabosho, the good; of Nenaubosho the evil—in her lisping Ojibway dialect that sounded like the softer voices of the forest.

At last the sudden subsidence of the waters; the splendid eager blossoming of the land into new leaves, lush grasses, an abandon of sweetbrier and hepatica. The air blew soft, a thousand singing birds sprang from the soil, the wild goose cried in triumph. Overhead shone the hot sun of the Northern summer.

From the wilderness came the *brigades* bearing their pelts, the hardy traders of the winter posts, striking hot the imagination through the mysterious and lonely allurement of their callings. For a brief season, transient as the flash of a loon's wing on the shadow of a lake, the post was bright with the thronging of many people. The Indians pitched their wigwams on the broad meadows below the bend; the half-breeds sauntered about, flashing bright teeth and wicked dark eyes at whom it might concern; the traders gazed stolidly over their little black pipes, and uttered brief sentences through their thick black beards. Everywhere was gay sound—the fiddle, the laugh, the song; everywhere was gay color—the red sashes of the *voyageurs*, the beaded moccasins and leggings of the *mètis*, the capotes of the *brigade*, the variegated costumes of the Crees and Ojibways. Like the wild roses around the edge of the muskegs, this brief flowering of the year passed. Again the nights were long, again the frost crept down from the eternal snow, again the wolves howled across barren wastes.

Just now the girl stood ankle-deep in green grasses, a bath of sunlight falling about her, a tingle of salt wind humming up the river from the bay's offing. She was clad in gray wool, and wore no hat. Her soft hair, the color of ripe wheat, blew about her temples, shadowing eyes of fathomless black. The wind had brought to the light and delicate brown of her complexion a trace of color to match her lips, whose scarlet did not fade after the ordinary and imperceptible manner into the tinge of her skin, but continued vivid to the very edge; her eyes were wide and unseeing. One hand rested idly on the breech of an ornamented bronze field-gun.

McDonald, the chief trader, passed from the house to the store where his bartering with the Indians was daily carried on; the other Scotchman in the Post, Galen Albret, her father, and the head Factor of all this region, paced back and forth across the veranda of the factory, caressing his white beard; up by the stockade, young Achille Picard tuned his whistle to the note of the curlew; across the meadow from the church wandered Crane, the little Church of England missionary, peering from short-sighted pale blue eyes; beyond the coulee, Sarnier and his Indians *chock-chock-chocked* away at the seams of the long coast-trading bateau. The girl saw nothing, heard nothing. She was dreaming, she was trying to remember.

In the lines of her slight figure, in its pose there by the old gun over the old, old river, was the grace of gentle blood, the pride of caste. Of all this region her father was the absolute lord, feared, loved, obeyed by all its human creatures. When he went abroad, he travelled in a state almost medieval in its magnificence; when he stopped at home, men came to him from the Albany, the Kenógami, the Missináibe, the Mattágami, the Abítibi—from all the rivers of the North—to receive his commands. Way was made for him, his lightest word was attended. In his house dwelt ceremony, and of his house she was the princess. Unconsciously she had taken the gracious habit of command. She had come to value her smile, her word, to value herself. The lady of a realm greater than the countries of Europe, she moved serene, pure, lofty amid dependants.

And as the lady of this realm she did honor to her father's guests—sitting stately behind the beautiful silver service, below the portrait of the Company's greatest explorer, Sir George Simpson, dispensing crude fare in gracious manner, listening silently to the conversation, finally withdrawing at the last with a sweeping courtesy to play soft, melancholy, and world-forgotten airs on the old piano, brought over years before by the *Lady Head*, while the guests made merry with the mellow port and ripe Manila cigars which the Company supplied its servants. Then coffee, still with her natural Old World charm of the *grande dame*. Such guests were not many, nor came often. There was McTavish of Rupert's House, a three days' journey to the northeast; Rand of Fort Albany, a week's travel to the northwest; Mault of Fort George, ten days beyond either, all grizzled in the Company's service. With them came their clerks, mostly English and Scotch younger sons, with a vast respect for the Company, and a vaster for their Factor's daughter. Once in two or three years appeared the inspectors from Winnipeg, true lords of the North, with their six-fathom canoes, their luxurious furs, their red banners trailing like gonfalons in the water. Then this post of Conjuror's House feasted and danced, undertook gay excursions, discussed in public or private conclave weighty matters, grave and reverend advices, cautions, and commands. They went. Desolation again crept in.

The girl dreamed. She was trying to remember. Far-off, half-forgotten visions of brave, courtly men, of gracious, beautiful women, peopled the clouds of her imaginings. She heard them again, as voices beneath the roar of rapids, like far-away bells tinkling faintly through a wind, pitying her, exclaiming over her; she saw them dim and changing, as wraiths of a fog, as shadow pictures in a mist beneath the moon, leaning to her with bright, shining eyes full of compassion for the little girl who was to go so far away into an unknown land; she felt them, as the touch of a breeze when the night is still, fondling her, clasping her, tossing her aloft in farewell. One she felt plainly—a gallant youth who held her up for all to see. One she saw clearly—a dewy-eyed, lovely woman who murmured loving, broken words. One she heard distinctly—a gentle voice that said, "God's love be with you, little one, for you have far to go, and many days to pass before you see Quebec again." And the girl's eyes suddenly swam bright, for the northland was very dreary. She threw her palms out in a gesture of weariness.

Then her arms dropped, her eyes widened, her head bent forward in the attitude of listening.

"Achille!" she called, "Achille! Come here!"

The young fellow approached respectfully.

"Mademoiselle?" he asked.

"Don't you hear?" she said.

Faint, between intermittent silences, came the singing of men's voices from the south.

"*Grace à Dieu!*" cried Achille. "Eet is so. Eet is dat *brigade!*"

He ran shouting toward the factory.

CHAPTER TWO

Men, women, dogs, children sprang into sight from nowhere and ran pell-mell to the two cannon. Galen Albret, reappearing from the factory, began to issue orders. Two men set about hoisting on the tall flag-staff the blood-red banner of the Company Speculation, excited and earnest, arose among the men as to which of the branches of the Moose this *brigade* had hunted—the Abítibi, the Mattágami, or the Missináibie. The half-breed women shaded their eyes. Mrs. Cockburn, the doctor's wife, and the only other white woman in the settlement, came and stood by Virginia Albret's side. Wishkobun, the Ojibway woman from the south country, and Virginia's devoted familiar, took her half-jealous stand on the other.

"It is the same every year. We always like to see them come," said Mrs. Cockburn, in her monotonous low voice of resignation.

"Yes," replied Virginia, moving a little impatiently, for she anticipated eagerly the picturesque coming of these men of the Silent Places, and wished to savor the pleasure undistracted.

"Mi-di-mo-yay ka'-win-ni-shi-shin," said Wishkobun, quietly.

"Ae," replied Virginia, with a little laugh, patting the woman's brown hand.

A shout arose. Around the bend shot a canoe. At once every paddle in it was raised to a perpendicular salute, then all together dashed into the water with the full strength of the *voyageurs* wielding them. The canoe fairly leaped through the cloud of spray. Another rounded the bend, another double row of paddles flashed in the sunlight, another crew, broke into a tumult of rapid exertion as they raced the last quarter mile of the long journey. A third burst into view, a fourth, a fifth. The silent river was alive with motion, glittering with color. The canoes swept onward, like race-horses straining against the rider. Now the spectators could make out plainly the boatmen. It could be seen that they had decked themselves out for the occasion. Their heads were bound with bright-colored fillets, their necks with gay scarves. The paddles were adorned with gaudy woollen streamers. New leggings, of holiday pattern, were intermittently visible on the bowsmen and steersmen as they half rose to give added force to their efforts.

At first the men sang their canoe songs, but as the swift rush of the birch-barks brought them almost to their journey's end, they burst into wild shrieks and whoops of delight.

All at once they were close to hand. The steersman rose to throw his entire weight on the paddle. The canoe swung abruptly for the shore. Those in it did not relax their exertions, but continued their vigorous strokes until within a few yards of apparent destruction.

"Holá! holá!" they cried, thrusting their paddles straight down into the water with a strong backward twist. The stout wood bent and cracked. The canoe stopped short and the *voyageurs* leaped ashore to be swallowed up in the crowd that swarmed down upon them.

The races were about equally divided, and each acted after its instincts—the Indian greeting his people quietly, and stalking away to the privacy of his wigwam; the more volatile white catching his wife or his sweetheart or his child to his arms. A swarm of Indian women and half-grown children set about unloading the canoes.

Virginia's eyes ran over the crews of the various craft. She recognized them all, of course, to the last Indian packer, for in so small a community the personality and doings of even the humblest members are well known to everyone. Long since she had identified the *brigade*. It was of the Missináibie, the great river whose head-waters rise a scant hundred feet from those that flow as many miles south into Lake Superior. It drains a wild and rugged country whose forests cling to bowlder hills, whose streams issue from deep-riven gorges, where for many years the big gray wolves had gathered in unusual abundance. She knew by heart the winter posts, although she had never seen them. She could imagine the isolation of such a place, and the intense loneliness of the solitary man condemned to live through the dark Northern winters, seeing no one but the rare Indians who might come in to trade with him for their pelts. She could appreciate the wild joy of a return for a brief season to the company of fellow-men.

When her glance fell upon the last of the canoes, it rested with a flash of surprise. The craft was still floating idly, its bow barely caught against the bank. The crew had deserted, but amidships, among the packages of pelts and duffel, sat a stranger. The canoe was that of the post at Kettle Portage.

She saw the stranger to be a young man with a clean-cut face, a trim athletic figure dressed in the complete costume of the *voyageurs*, and thin brown and muscular hands. When the canoe touched the bank he had taken no part in the scramble to shore, and so had sat forgotten and unnoticed save by the girl, his figure erect with something of the Indian's stoical indifference. Then when, for a moment, he imagined himself free from observation, his expression abruptly changed. His hands clenched tense between his buckskin knees, his eyes glanced here and there restlessly, and an indefinable shadow of something which Virginia felt herself obtuse in labelling desperation, and yet to which she discovered it impossible to fit a name, descended on his features, darkening them. Twice he glanced away to the south. Twice he ran his eye over the vociferating crowd on the narrow beach.

Absorbed in the silent drama of a man's unguarded expression, Virginia leaned forward eagerly. In some vague manner it was borne in on her that once before she had experienced the same emotion, had come into contact with someone, something, that had affected her emotionally just as this man did now. But she could not place it. Over and over again she forced her mind to the very point of recollection, but always it slipped back again from the verge of attainment. Then a little movement, some thrust forward of the head, some nervous, rapid shifting of the hands or feet, some unconscious poise of the shoulders, brought the scene flashing before her—the white snow, the still forest, the little square pen-trap, the wolverine, desperate but cool, thrusting its blunt nose quickly here and there in baffled hope of an orifice of escape. Somehow the man reminded her of the animal, the fierce little woods marauder, trapped and hopeless, but scorning to cower as would the gentler creatures of the forest.

Abruptly his expression changed again. His figure stiffened, the muscles of his face turned iron. Virginia saw that someone on the beach had pointed toward him. His mask was on.

The first burst of greeting was over. Here and there one of

another of the *brigade* members jerked their heads in the stranger's direction, explaining low-voiced to their companions. Soon all eyes turned curiously toward the canoe. A hum of low-voiced comment took the place of louder delight.

The stranger, finding himself generally observed, rose slowly to his feet, picked his way with a certain exaggerated deliberation of movement over the duffel lying in the bottom of the canoe, until he reached the bow, where he paused, one foot lifted to the gunwale just above the emblem of the painted star. Immediately a dead silence fell. Groups shifted, drew apart, and together again, like the slow agglomeration of sawdust on the surface of water, until at last they formed in a semicircle of staring, whose centre was the bow of the canoe and the stranger from Kettle Portage. The men scowled, the women regarded him with a half-fearful curiosity.

Virginia Albret shivered in the shock of this sudden electric polarity. The man seemed alone against a sullen, unexplained hostility. The desperation she had thought to read but a moment before had vanished utterly, leaving in its place a scornful indifference and perhaps more than a trace of recklessness. He was ripe for an outbreak. She did not in the least understand, but she knew it from the depths of her woman's instinct, and unconsciously her sympathies flowed out to this man, alone without a greeting where all others came to their own.

For perhaps a full sixty seconds the new-comer stood uncertain what he should do, or perhaps waiting for some word or act to tip the balance of his decision. One after another those on shore felt the insolence of his stare, and shifted uneasily. Then his deliberate scrutiny rose to the group by the cannon. Virginia caught her breath sharply. In spite of herself she could not turn away. The stranger's eye crossed her own. She saw the hard look fade into pleased surprise. Instantly his hat swept the gunwale of the canoe. He stepped magnificently ashore. The crisis was over. Not a word had been spoken.

CHAPTER THREE

Galen Albret sat in his rough-hewn arm-chair at the head of the table, receiving the reports of his captains. The long, narrow room opened before him, heavy raftered, massive, white, with a cavernous fireplace at either end. Above him frowned Sir George's portrait, at his right hand and his left stretched the row of home-made heavy chairs, finished smooth and dull by two centuries of use.

His arms were laid along the arms of his seat; his shaggy head was sunk forward until his beard swept the curve of his big chest; the heavy tufts of hair above his eyes were drawn steadily together in a frown of attention. One after another the men arose and spoke. He made no movement, gave no sign, his short, powerful form blotted against the lighter silhouette of his chair, only his eyes and the white of his beard gleaming out of the dusk.

Kern of Old Brunswick House, Achard of New; Ki-wa-nee, the Indian of Flying Post—these and others told briefly of many things, each in his own language. To all Galen Albret listened in silence. Finally Louis Placide from the post at Kettle Portage got to his feet. He too reported of the trade,—so many "beaver" of tobacco, of powder, of lead, of pork, of flour, of tea, given in exchange; so many mink, otter, beaver, ermine, marten, and fisher pelts taken in return. Then he paused and went on at greater length in regard to the stranger, speaking evenly but with emphasis. When he had finished, Galen Albret struck a bell at his elbow. Me-en-gan, the bowsman of the Factor's canoe, entered, followed closely by the young man who had that afternoon arrived.

He was dressed still in his costume of the *voyageur*—the loose blouse shirt, the buckskin leggings and moccasins, the long tasselled red sash. His head was as high and his glance as free, but now the steel blue of his eye had become steady and wary, and two faint lines had traced themselves between his brows. At his entrance a hush of expectation fell. Galen Albret did not stir, but the others hitched nearer the long, narrow table, and two or three leaned both elbows on it the better to catch what should ensue.

Me-en-gan stopped by the door, but the stranger walked

steadily the length of the room until he faced the Factor. Then he paused and waited collectedly for the other to speak.

This the Factor did not at once begin to do, but sat impassive—apparently without thought—while the heavy breathing of the men in the room marked off the seconds of time. Finally abruptly Galen Albret's cavernous voice boomed forth. Something there was strangely mysterious, cryptic, in the virile tones issuing from a bulk so massive and inert. Galen Albret did not move, did not even raise the heavy-lidded, dull stare of his eyes to the young man who stood before him; hardly did his broad arched chest seem to rise and fall with the respiration of speech; and yet each separate word leaped forth alive, instinct with authority.

"Once at Leftfoot Lake, two Indians caught you asleep," he pronounced. "They took your pelts and arms, and escorted you to Sudbury. They were my Indians. Once on the upper Abítibi you were stopped by a man named Herbert, who warned you from the country, after relieving you of your entire outfit. He told you on parting what you might expect if you should repeat the attempt—severe measures, the severest. Herbert was my man. Now Louis Placide surprises you in a rapids near Kettle Portage and brings you here."

During the slow delivering of these accurately spaced words, the attitude of the men about the long, narrow table gradually changed. Their curiosity had been great before, but now their intellectual interest was awakened, for these were facts of which Louis Placide's statement had given no inkling. Before them, for the dealing, was a problem of the sort whose solution had earned for Galen Albret a reputation in the north country. They glanced at one another to obtain the sympathy of attention, then back toward their chief in anxious expectation of his next words. The stranger, however, remained unmoved. A faint smile had sketched the outline of his lips when first the Factor began to speak. This smile he maintained to the end. As the older man paused, he shrugged his shoulders.

"All of that is quite true," he admitted.

Even the unimaginative men of the Silent Places started at these simple words, and vouchsafed to their speaker a more sympathetic attention. For the tones in which they were delivered possessed that deep, rich throat timbre which so often means power—personal magnetism—deep, from the chest, with vibrant throat tones suggesting a volume of sound which may in fact be only hinted by the loudness the man at the moment sees fit to employ. Such a voice is a responsive instrument on which emotion and mood play wonderfully seductive strains.

"All of that is quite true," he repeated after a second's pause; "but what has it to do with me? Why am I stopped and sent out from the free forest? I am really curious to know your excuse."

"This," replied Galen Albret, weightily, "is my domain. I tolerate no rivalry here."

"Your right?" demanded the young man, briefly.

"I have made the trade, and I intend to keep it."

"In other words, the strength of your good right arm," supplemented the stranger, with the faintest hint of a sneer.

"That is neither here nor there," rejoined Galen Albret, "the point is that I intend to keep it. I've had you sent out, but you have been too stupid or too obstinate to take the hint. Now I have to warn you in person. I shall send you out once more, but this time you must promise me not to meddle with the trade again."

He paused for a response. The young man's smile merely became accentuated.

"I have means of making my wishes felt," warned the Factor.

"Quite so," replied the young man, deliberately, "*La Longue Traverse.*"

At this unexpected pronouncement of that dread name two of the men swore violently; the others thrust back their chairs and sat, their arms rigidly braced against the table's edge, staring wide-eyed and open-mouthed at the speaker. Only Galen Albret remained unmoved.

"What do you mean by that?" he asked, calmly.

"It amuses you to be ignorant," replied the stranger, with some contempt. "Don't you think this farce is about played out? I do. If you think you're deceiving me any with this show of formality, you're mightily mistaken. Don't you suppose I knew what I was about when I came into this country? Don't you suppose I had weighed the risks and had made up my mind to take my medicine if I should be caught? Your methods are not quite so secret as you imagine. I know perfectly well what happens to Free Traders in Rupert's Land."

"You seem very certain of your information."

"Your men seem equally so," pointed out the stranger.

Galen Albret, at the beginning of the young man's longer speech, had sunk almost immediately into his passive calm—the calm of great elemental bodies, the calm of a force so vast as to rest motionless by the very static power of its mass. When he spoke again, it was in the tentative manner of his earlier interrogatory, committing himself not at all, seeking to plumb his opponent's knowledge.

"Why, if you have realized the gravity of your situation have you persisted after having been twice warned?" he inquired.

"Because you're not the boss of creation," replied the young man, bluntly.

Galen Albret merely raised his eyebrows.

"I've got as much business in this country as you have," continued the young man, his tone becoming more incisive. "You don't seem to realize that your charter of monopoly has expired. If the government was worth a damn it would see to you fellows. You have no more right to order me out of here than I would have to order you out. Suppose some old Husky up on Whale River should send you word that you weren't to trap in the Whale River district next winter. I'll bet you'd be there. You Hudson Bay men tried the same game out west. It didn't work. You ask your western men if they ever heard of Ned Trent."

"Your success does not seem to have followed you here," suggested the Factor, ironically.

The young man smiled.

"This *Longue Traverse*," went on Albret, "what is your idea there? I have heard something of it. What is your information?"

Ned Trent laughed outright. "You don't imagine there is any secret about that!" he marvelled. "Why, every child north of the Line knows that. You will send me away without arms, and with but a handful of provisions. If the wilderness and starvation fail, your runners will not. I shall never reach the Temiscamingues alive."

"The same old legend," commented Galen Albret in apparent

amusement, "I heard it when I first came to this country. You'll find a dozen such in every Indian camp."

"Jo Bagneau, Morris Proctor, John May, William Jarvis," checked off the young man on his fingers.

"Personal enmity," replied the Factor.

He glanced up to meet the young man's steady, sceptical smile.

"You do not believe me?"

"Oh, if it amuses you," conceded the stranger.

"The thing is not even worth discussion."

"Remarkable sensation among our friends here for so idle a tale."

Galen Albret considered.

"You will remember that throughout you have forced this interview," he pointed out. "Now I must ask your definite promise to get out of this country and to stay out."

"No," replied Ned Trent.

"Then a means shall be found to make you!" threatened the Factor, his anger blazing at last.

"Ah," said the stranger softly.

Galen Albret raised his hand and let it fall. The bronzed and gaudily bedecked men filed out.

CHAPTER FOUR

In the open air the men separated in quest of their various families or friends. The stranger lingered undecided for a moment on the top step of the veranda, and then wandered down the little street, if street it could be called where horses there were none. On the left ranged the square whitewashed houses with their dooryards, the old church, the workshop. To the right was a broad grass-plot, and then the Moose, slipping by to the distant offing. Over a little bridge the stranger idled, looking curiously about him. The great trading-house attracted his attention, with its narrow picket lane leading to the door; the storehouse surrounded by a protective log fence; the fort itself, a medley of heavy-timbered stockades and square block-houses. After a moment he resumed his strolling. Everywhere he went the people looked at him, ceasing their varied occupations. No one spoke to him, no one hindered him. To all intents and purposes he was as free as the air. But all about the island flowed the barrier of the Moose, and beyond frowned the wilderness—strong as iron bars to an unarmed man.

Brooding on his imprisonment the Free Trader forgot his surroundings. The post, the river, the forest, the distant bay faded from his sight, and he fell into deep reflection. There remained nothing of physical consciousness but a sense of the grateful spring warmth from the declining sun. At length he became vaguely aware of something else. He glanced up. Right by him he saw a handsome French half-breed sprawled out in the sun against a building, looking him straight in the face and flashing up at him a friendly smile.

"Hullo," said Achille Picard, "you mus' been 'sleep. I call you two t'ree tam."

The prisoner seemed to find something grateful in the greeting even from the enemy's camp. Perhaps it merely happened upon the psychological moment for a response.

"Hullo," he returned, and seated himself by the man's side, lazily stretching himself in enjoyment of the reflected heat.

"You is come off Kettle Portage, eh," said Achille, "I t'ink so. You is come trade dose fur? Eet is bad beez-ness, dis Conjur'

House. Ole' man he no lak' dat you trade dose fur. He's very hard, dat ole man."

"Yes," replied the stranger, "he has got to be, I suppose. This is the country of *la Longue Traverse*."

"I beleef you," responded Achille, cheerfully; "w'at you call heem your nam'?"

"Ned Trent."

"Me Achille—Achille Picard. I capitaine of dose dogs on dat winter *brigade*."

"It is a hard post. The winter travel is pretty tough."

"I beleef you."

"Better to take *la Longue Traverse* in summer, eh?"

"*La Longue Traverse—hees not mattaire w'en yo tak' heem*."

"Right you are. Have there been men sent out since you came here?"

"*Bâ oui*. Wan, two, t'ree. I don' remember. I t'ink Jo Bagneau Nobodee he don' know, but dat ole man an' hees *coureurs du bois* He ees wan ver' great man. Nobodee is know w'at he will do."

"I'm due to hit that trail myself, I suppose," said Ned Trent.

"I have t'ink so," acknowledged Achille, still with a tone of most engaging cheerfulness.

"Shall I be sent out at once, do you think?"

"I don' know. Sometam' dat ole man ver' queek. Sometam' he ver' slow. One day Injun mak' heem ver' mad; he let heem go, and shot dat Injun right off. Noder tam he get mad on one *voyageur*, but he don' keel heem queek; he bring heem here, mak' heem stay in dose warm room, feed heem dose plaintee grub. Purty soon dose *voyageur* is get fat, is go sof; he no good for dose trail. Ole man he mak' heem go ver' far off, mos' to Whale Reever. Eet is plaintee cole. Dat *voyageur*, he freeze to hees inside. Dey tell me he feex heem like dat."

"Achille, you haven't anything against me—do you want me to die?"

The half-breed flashed his white teeth.

"*Bâ non*," he replied, carelessly. "For w'at I want dat you die? I t'ink you bus' up bad; *vous avez la mauvaise fortune*."

"Listen. I have nothing with me; but out at the front I am very rich. I will give you a hundred dollars, if you will help me to get away."

"I can' do eet," smiled Picard.

"Why not?"

"Ole man he fin' dat out. He is wan devil, dat ole man. I lak firs'-rate help you; I lak' dat hundred dollar. On Ojibway countree dey make hees nam' *Wagosh*—dat mean fox. He know everyt'ing."

"I'll make it two hundred—three hundred—five hundred."

"W'at you wan' me do?" hesitated Achille Picard at the last figure.

"Get me a rifle and some cartridges."

The half-breed rolled a cigarette, lighted it, and inhaled a deep breath.

"I can' do eet," he declared. "I can' do eet for t'ousand dollar—ten t'ousand. I don't t'ink you fin' anywan on dis settle-ment w'at can dare do eet. He is wan devil. He's count all de carabine on dis pos', an' w'en he is mees wan, he fin' out purty queek who is tak' heem."

"Steal one from someone else," suggested Trent.

"He fin' out jess sam'," objected the half-breed, obstinately. "You don' know heem. He mak' you geev yourself away, when he lak' do dat." The smile had left the man's face. This was evidently too serious a matter to be taken lightly.

"Well, come with me, then," urged Ned Trent, with some impatience. "A thousand dollars I'll give you. With that you can be rich somewhere else."

But the man was becoming more and more uneasy, glancing furtively from left to right and back again, in an evident panic lest the conversation be overheard, although the nearest dwelling-house was a score of yards distant.

"Hush," he whispered. "You mustn't talk lak' dat. Dose ole man fin' you out. You can' hide away from heem. Ole tam long ago, Pierre Cadotte is stole feefteen skin of de otter—de sea-otter—and he is sol' dem on Winnipeg. He is get 'bout t'ousand beaver—five hunder' dollar. Den he is mak' dose longue voyage wes'—ver' far wes'—*on dit* Peace Reever. He is mak' heem dose cabane, w'ere he is leev long tam wid wan man of Mackenzie. He is call it hees nam' Dick Henderson. I is meet Dick Henderson on Winnipeg las' year, w'en I mak' paddle on dem Factor Brigade, an' dose High Commissionaire. He is tol' me wan night pret' late he wake up all de queeck he can w'en he is hear wan noise in dose cabane, an' he is see wan Injun, lak' phantome 'gainst de moon to de door. Dick Henderson he is 'sleep, he don' know w'at he mus' do. Does Injun is step ver' sof' an' go on bunk of Pierre Cadotte. Pierre Cadotte is mak' de beeg cry. Dick Henderson say he no see dose Injun no more, an' he fin' de door shut. *Bâ* Pierre Cadotte, she's go dead. He is mak' wan beeg hole in hees ches'."

"Some enemy, some robber frightened away because the Henderson man woke up, probably," suggested Ned Trent.

The half-breed laid his hand impressively on the other's arm and leaned forward until his bright black eyes were within a foot of the other's face.

"W'en dose Injun is stan' heem in de moonlight, Dick Henderson is see hees face. Dick Henderson is know all dose Injun. He is tole me dat Injun is not Peace Reever Injun. Dick Henderson is say dose Injun is Ojibway Injun—Ojibway Injun two t'ousand mile wes'—on Peace Reever! Dat's curi's!"

"I was tell you nodder story—" went on Achille, after a moment.

"Never mind," interrupted the Trader. "I believe you."

"Maybee," said Achille cheerfully, "you stan' some show—not moche—eef he sen' you out pret' queeck. Does small *perdrix* is yonge, an' dose duck. Maybee you is catch dem, maybee you is keel dem wit' bow an' arrow. Dat's not beeg chance. You mus' geev dose *coureurs de bois* de sleep w'en you arrive. *Voilà*, I geev you my knife!"

He glanced rapidly to right and left, then slipped a small object into the stranger's hand.

"*Bâ*, I t'ink does ole man is know dat. I t'ink he kip you here till tam w'en dose *perdrix* and duck is all grow up beeg' nuff so he can fly."

"I'm not watched," said the young man in eager tones; "I'll slip away tonight."

"Dat no good," objected Picard. "W'at you do? S'pose you do dat, dose *coureurs* keel you *toute suite*. Dey is have good excuse, an' you is have nothing to mak' de fight. You sleep away, and dose ole man is sen' out plaintee Injun. Dey is fine you sure. *Bâ*, eef he *sen'* you out, den he sen' onlee two Injun. Maybee you fight dem; I don' know. *Non, mon ami*, eef you is wan' get away w'en dose ole man he don' know eet, you mus' have dose carabine. Den you is have wan leetle chance. *Bâ*, eef you is not have heem dose carabine, you mus' need dose leetle grub he geev you, and not plaintee Injun follow you, onlee two."

"And I cannot get the rifle."

"An' dose ole man is don' sen' you out till eet is too late for mak' de grub on de fores'. Dat's w'at I t'ink. Dat ees not fonny for you."

Ned Trent's eyes were almost black with thought. Suddenly he threw his head up.

"I'll make him send me out now," he asserted confidently.

"How you mak' eet him?"

"I'll talk turkey to him till he's so mad he can't see straight. Then maybe he'll send me out right away."

"How you mak' eet him so mad?" inquired Picard, with mild curiosity.

"Never you mind—I'll do it."

"*Bâ oui*," ruminated Picard, "He is get mad pret' queeck. I t'ink p'raps dat plan he go all right. You was get heem mad plaintee easy. Den maybee he is sen' you out *toute suite*—maybee he is shoot you."

"I'll take the chances—my friend."

"*Bâ oui*," shrugged Achille Picard, "eet is wan chance."

He commenced to roll another cigarette.

CHAPTER FIVE

Having sat buried in thought for a full five minutes after the traders of the winter posts had left him, Galen Albret thrust back his chair and walked into a room, long, low, and heavily raftered, strikingly unlike the Council Room. Its floor was overlaid with dark rugs; a piano of ancient model filled one corner; pictures and books broke the wall; the lamps and the windows were shaded; a woman's work-basket and a tea-set occupied a large table. Only a certain barbaric profusion of furs, the huge fireplace, and the rough rafters of the ceiling differentiated the place from the drawing-room of a well-to-do family anywhere.

Galen Albret sank heavily into a chair and struck a bell. A tall, slightly stooped English servant, with correct side whiskers and incompetent, watery blue eyes, answered. To him said the Factor:

"I wish to see Miss Albret."

A moment later Virginia entered the room.

"Let us have some tea, O-mi-mi," requested her father.

The girl moved gently about, preparing and lighting the lamp, measuring the tea, her fair head bowed gracefully over her task, her dark eyes pensive and but half following what she did. Finally with a certain air of decision she seated herself on the arm of a chair.

"Father," said she.

"Yes."

"A stranger came today with Louis Placide of Kettle Portage."

"Well?"

"He was treated strangely by our people, and he treated them strangely in return. Why is that?"

"Who can tell?"

"What is his station? Is he a common trader? He does not look it."

"He is a man of intelligence and daring."

"Then why is he not our guest?"

Galen Albret did not answer. After a moment's pause he asked again for his tea. The girl turned away impatiently. Here was a puzzle, neither the *voyageurs*, nor Wishkobun her nurse, nor her father would explain to her. The first had grinned stupidly; the second had drawn her shawl across her face, the third asked for tea!

She handed her father the cup, hesitated, then ventured to inquire whether she was forbidden to greet the stranger should the occasion arise.

"He is a gentleman," replied her father.

She sipped her tea thoughtfully, her imagination stirring. Again her recollection lingered over the clear bronze lines of the stranger's face. Something vaguely familiar seemed to touch her consciousness with ghostly fingers. She closed her eyes and tried to clutch them. At once they were withdrawn. And then again, when her attention wandered, they stole back, plucking appealingly at the hem of her recollections.

The room was heavy-curtained, deep embrasured, for the house, beneath its clap-boards, was of logs. Although out of doors the clear spring sunshine still flooded the valley of the Moose; within, the shadows had begun with velvet fingers to extinguish the brighter lights. Virginia threw herself back on a chair in the corner.

"Virginia," said Galen Albret, suddenly.

"Yes, father."

"You are no longer a child, but a woman. Would you like to go to Quebec?"

She did not answer him at once, but pondered beneath close-knit brows.

"Do you wish me to go, father?" she asked at length.

"You are eighteen. It is time you saw the world, time you learned the ways of other people. But the journey is hard. I may not see you again for some years. You go among strangers."

He fell silent again. Motionless he had been, except for the mumbling of his lips beneath his beard.

"It shall be just as you wish," he added a moment later.

At once a conflict arose in the girl's mind between her restless dreams and her affections. But beneath all the glitter of the question there was really nothing to take her out. Here was her father, here were the things she loved; yonder was novelty—and loneliness.

Her existence at Conjuror's House was perhaps a little complex, but it was familiar. She knew the people, and she took a daily and unwearying delight in the kindness and simplicity of their bearing toward herself. Each detail of life came to her in the round of habit, wearing the garment of accustomed use. But of the world she knew nothing except what she had been able to body forth from her reading, and that had merely given her imagination something tangible with which to feed her self-distrust.

"Must I decide at once?" she asked.

"If you go this year, it must be with the Abítibi *brigade*. You have until then."

"Thank you, father," said the girl, sweetly.

The shadows stole their surroundings one by one, until only the bright silver of the tea-service, and the glitter of polished wood, and the square of the open door remained. Galen Albret became an inert dark mass. Virginia's gray was lost in that of the twilight.

Time passed. The clock ticked on. Faintly sounds penetrated from the kitchen, and still more faintly from out of doors. Then the rectangle of the doorway was darkened by a man peering uncertainly. The man wore his hat, from which slanted a slender heron's plume; his shoulders were square; his thighs slim and graceful. Against the light, one caught the outline of the sash's tassel and the fringe of his leggings.

"Are you there, Galen Albret?" he challenged.

The spell of twilight mystery broke. It seemed as if suddenly the air had become surcharged with the vitality of opposition.

"What then?" countered the Factor's heavy, deliberate tones.

"True, I see you now," rejoined the visitor carelessly, as he flung himself across the arm of a chair and swung one foot. "I do not doubt you are convinced by this time of my intention."

"My recollection does not tell me what messenger I sent to ask this interview."

"Correct," laughed the young man a little hardly. "You *didn't* ask it. I attended to that myself. What *you* want doesn't concern me in the least. What do you suppose I care what, or what not, any of this crew wants? I'm master of my own ideas, anyway, thank God. If you don't like what I do, you can always stop me." In the tone of his voice was a distinct challenge. Galen Albret, it seemed, chose to pass it by.

"True," he replied sombrely, after a barely perceptible pause to mark his tacit displeasure. "It is your hour. Say on."

"I should like to know the date at which I take *la Longue Traverse*".

"You persist in that nonsense?"

"Call my departure whatever you want to—I have the name for it. When do I leave?"

"I have not decided."

"And in the meantime?"

"Do as you please."

"Ah, thanks for this generosity," cried the young man, in a tone of declamatory sarcasm so artificial as fairly to scent the elocutionary. "To do as I please—here—now there's a blessed privilege! I may walk around where I want to, talk to such as have a good word for me, punish those who have not! But do I err in concluding that the state of your game law is such that it would be useless to reclaim my rifle from the engaging Placide?"

"You have a fine instinct," approved the Factor.

"It is one of my valued possessions," rejoined the young man, insolently. He struck a match, and by its light selected a cigarette.

"I do not myself use tobacco in this room," suggested the older speaker.

"I am curious to learn the limits of your forbearance," replied the younger, proceeding to smoke.

He threw back his head and regarded his opponent with an open challenge, daring him to become angry. The match went out.

Virginia, who had listened in growing anger and astonishment, unable longer to refrain from defending the dignity of her usually autocratic father, although he seemed little disposed to defend himself, now intervened from her dark corner on the divan.

"Is the journey then so long, sir," she asked composedly, "that it at once inspires such anticipations—and such bitterness?"

In an instant the man was on his feet, hat in hand, and the cigarette had described a fiery curve into the empty hearth.

"I beg your pardon, sincerely," he cried, "I did not know you were here!"

"You might better apologize to my father," replied Virginia.

The young man stepped forward and, without asking permission, lighted one of the tall lamps.

"The lady of the guns!" he marvelled softly to himself.

He moved across the room, looking down on her inscrutably, while she looked up at him in composed expectation of an apology—and Galen Albret sat motionless, in the shadow of his great arm-chair. But after a moment her calm attention broke down. Something there was about this man that stirred her emotions—whether of curiosity, pity, indignation, or a slight defensive fear she was not introspective enough to care to inquire. And yet the sensation was not altogether unpleasant, and, as at the guns that afternoon, a certain portion of her consciousness remained in sympathy with whatever it was of mysterious attraction he represented to her. In him she felt the dominant, as a wild creature of the woods instinctively senses the master and drops its eyes. Resentment did not leave her, but over it spread a film of confusion that robbed it of its potency. In him, in his mood, in his words, in his manner, was something that called out in direct appeal the more primitive instincts hitherto dormant beneath her sense of maidenhood, so that even at this vexed moment of conscious opposition, her heart was ranging itself on his side. Overpoweringly the feeling swept her that she was not acting in accordance with her sense of fitness. She knew she should strike, but was unable to give due force to the blow. In the confusion of such a discovery, her eyelids fluttered and fell. And he saw, and, understanding his power, dropped swiftly beside her on the broad divan.

"You must pardon me, mademoiselle," he begun, his voice sinking to a depth of rich music singularly caressing. "To you I may seem to have small excuses, but when a man is vouchsafed a glimpse of heaven only to be cast out the next instant into hell, he is not always particular in the choice of words."

All the time his eyes sought hers, which avoided the challenge, and the strong masculine charm of magnetism which he possessed in such vital abundance overwhelmed her unaccustomed consciousness. Galen Albret shifted uneasily, and shot a glance in their direction. The stranger, perceiving this, lowered his voice in register and tone, and went on with almost exaggerated earnestness.

"Surely you can forgive me, a desperate man, almost anything?"

"I do not understand," said Virginia, with a palpable effort.

Ned Trent leaned forward until his eager face was almost at her shoulder.

"Perhaps not," he urged; "I cannot ask you to try. But suppose, mademoiselle, you were in my case. Suppose your eyes—like mine—have rested on nothing but a howling wilderness for dear heaven knows how long; you come at last in sight of real houses, real grass, real dooryard gardens just ready to blossom in the spring, real food, real beds, real books, real men with whom to exchange the sensible word, and something more, mademoiselle—a woman such as one dreams of in the long forest nights under the stars. And you know that while others, the lucky ones, may stay to enjoy it all, you, the unfortunate, are condemned to leave it at any moment for *la Longue Traverse*. Would not you, too, be bitter, mademoiselle? Would not you too mock and sneer? Think, mademoiselle, I have not even the little satisfaction of rousing men's anger. I can insult them as I will, but they turn aside in pity, saying one to another: 'Let us pleasure him in this, poor fellow, for he is about to take *la Longue Traverse*.' That is why your father accepts calmly from me what he would not from another."

Virginia sat bolt upright on the divan, her hands clasped in her lap, her wonderful black eyes looking straight out before her, trying to avoid her companion's insistent gaze. His attention was fixed on her mobile and changing countenance, but he marked with evident satisfaction Galen Albret's growing uneasiness. This was evidenced only by a shifting of the feet, a tapping of the fingers, a turning of the shaggy head—in such a man slight tokens are significant. The silence deepened with the shadows drawing about the single lamp, while Virginia attempted to maintain a breathing advantage above the flood of strange emotions which the personality of this man had swept down upon her.

"It does not seem—" objected the girl in bewilderment, "I do not know—men are often out in this country for years at a time.

Long journeys are not unknown among us. We are used to under-taking them."

"But not *la Longue Traverse*," insisted the young man, som-brely.

"*La Longue Traverse*," she repeated in sweet perplexity.

"Sometimes called the Journey of Death," he explained.

She turned to look him in the eyes, a vague expression of puz-zled fear on her face.

"She has never heard of it," said Ned Trent to himself, and aloud: "Men who undertake it leave comfort behind. They em-brace hunger and weariness, cold and disease. At the last they embrace death, and are glad of his coming."

Something in his tone compelled belief; something in his face told her that he was a man by whom the inevitable hardships of winter and summer travel, fearful as they are, would be lightly endured. She shuddered.

"This dreadful thing is necessary?" she asked.

"Alas, yes."

"I do not understand—"

"In the North few of us understand," agreed the young man with a hint of bitterness seeping through his voice. "The mighty order, and so we obey. But that is beside the point. I have not told you these things to harrow you; I have tried to excuse myself for my actions. Does it touch you a little? Am I forgiven?"

"I do not understand how such things can be," she objected in some confusion, "why such journeys must exist. My mind cannot comprehend your explanations."

The stranger leaned forward abruptly, his eyes blazing with the magnetic personality of the man.

"But your heart?" he breathed.

It was the moment. "My heart—" she repeated, as though bewildered by the intensity of his eyes, "my heart—ah—yes!"

Immediately the blood rushed over her face and throat in a torrent. She snatched her eyes away, and cowered back in the corner, going red and white by turns, now angry, now frightened, now bewildered, until his gaze, half masterful, half pleading, again conquered hers. Galen Albret had ceased tapping his chair. In the dim light he sat, staring straight before him, massive, inert, grim.

"I believe you—" she murmured hurriedly at last. "I pity you!"

She rose. Quick as light he barred her passage.

"Don't! don't!" she pleaded. "I must go—you have shaken me—I—I do not understand myself—"

"I must see you again," he whispered eagerly. "Tonight—by the guns."

"No, no!"

"Tonight," he insisted.

She raised her eyes to his, this time naked of defence, so that the man saw down through their depths into her very soul.

"Oh," she begged, quivering, "let me pass. Don't you see—I'm going to cry!"

CHAPTER SIX

For a moment Ned Trent stared through the darkness into which Virginia had disappeared. Then he turned a troubled face to the task he had set himself, for the unexpectedly pathetic results of his fantastic attempt had shaken him. Twice he half turned as though to follow her. Then shaking his shoulders he bent his attention to the old man in the shadow of the chair.

He was given no opportunity for further speech, however, for at the sound of the closing door Galen Albret's impassivity had fallen from him. He sprang to his feet. The whole aspect of the man suddenly became electric, terrible. His eyes blazed; his heavy brows drew spasmodically toward each other; his jaws worked, twisting his beard into strange contortions; his massive frame straightened formidably; and his voice rumbled from the arch of his deep chest in a torrent of passionate sound.

"By God, young man!" he thundered, "you go too far! Take heed! I will not stand this! Do not you presume to make love to my daughter before my eyes!"

And Ned Trent, just within the dusky circle of lamplight, where the bold, sneering lines of his face stood out in relief against the twilight of the room, threw back his head and laughed. It was a clear laugh, but low, and in it were all the devils of triumph, and of insolence. Where the studied insult of words had failed, this single cachinnation succeeded. The Trader saw his opponent's eyes narrow. For a moment he thought the Factor was about to spring on him.

Then, with an effort that blackened his face with blood, Galen Albret controlled himself, and fell to striking the call-bell violently and repeatedly with the palm of his hand. After a moment Matthews, the English servant, came running in. To him the Factor was at first physically unable to utter a syllable. Then finally he managed to ejaculate the name of his bowsman with such violence of gesture that the frightened servant comprehended by sheer force of terror and ran out again in search of Me-en-gan.

This supreme effort seemed to clear the way for speech. Galen Albret began to address his opponent hoarsely in quick, disjointed sentences, a gasp for breath between each.

"You revived an old legend—*la Longue Traverse*—the myth. It shall be real—to—you—I will make it so. By God, you shall not defy me—"

Ned Trent smiled. "You do not deceive me," he rejoined, coolly.

"Silence!" cried the Factor. "Silence!—You shall speak no more!—You have said enough—"

Me-en-gan glided into the room. Galen Albret at once addressed him in the Ojibway language, gaining control of himself as he went on.

"Listen to me well," he commanded. "You shall make a count of all rifles in this place—at once. Let no one furnish this man with food or arms. You know the story of *la Longue Traverse*. This man shall take it. So inform my people. I, the Factor, decree it so. Prepare all things at once—understand, *at once*!"

Ned Trent waited to hear no more, but sauntered from the room whistling gayly a boatman's song. His point was gained.

Outside, the long Northern twilight with its beautiful shadows of crimson was descending from the upper regions of the east. A light wind breathed up-river from the bay. The Free Trader drew his lungs full of the evening air.

"Just the same, I think she will come," said he to himself. "*La Longue Traverse*, even at once, is a pretty slim chance. But this second string to my bow is better. I believe I'll get the rifle—if she comes!"

CHAPTER SEVEN

Virginia ran quickly up the narrow stairs to her own room, where she threw herself on the bed and buried her face in the pillows.

As she had said, she was very much shaken. And, too, she was afraid.

She could not understand. Heretofore she had moved among the men around her, pure, lofty, serene. Now at one blow all this crumbled. The stranger had outraged her finer feelings. He had insulted her father in her very presence;—for this she was angry. He had insulted herself;—for this she was afraid. He had demanded that she meet him again; but this—at least in the manner he had suggested—should not happen. And yet she confessed to herself a delicious wonder as to what he would do next, and a vague desire to see him again in order to find out. That she could not successfully combat this feeling made her angry at herself. And so in mingled fear, pride, anger, and longing she remained until Wishkobun, the Indian woman, glided in to dress her for the dinner whose formality she and her father consistently maintained. She fell to talking the soft Ojibway dialect, and in the conversation forgot some of her emotion and regained some of her calm.

Her surface thoughts, at least, were compelled for the moment to occupy themselves with other things. The Indian woman had to tell her of the silver fox brought in by Mu-hi-ken, an Indian of her own tribe; of the retort Achille Picard had made when MacLane had taunted him; of the forest fire that had declared itself far to the east, and of the theories to account for it where no campers had been. Yet underneath the rambling chatter Virginia was aware of something new in her consciousness, something delicious but as yet vague. In the gayest moment of her half-jesting, half-affectionate gossip with the Indian woman, she felt its uplift catching her breath from beneath, so that for the tiniest instant she would pause as though in readiness for some message which nevertheless delayed. A fresh delight in the present moment held her, a fresh anticipation of the immediate future, though both delight and anticipation were based on something without her knowledge. That would come later.

The sound of rapid footsteps echoed across the lower hall, a whistle ran into an air, sung gayly, with spirit:

> *"J'ai perdu ma maîtresse,*
> *Sans l'avoir merité,*
> *Pour un bouquet de roses*
> *Que je lui refusai.*
> *Li ya longtemps que je t'aime,*
> *Jamais je ne t'oublierai!"*

She fell abruptly silent, and spoke no more until she descended to the council-room where the table was now spread for dinner.

Two silver candlesticks lit the place. The men were waiting for her when she entered, and at once took their seats in the worn, rude chairs. White linen and glittering silver adorned the service, Galen Albret occupied one end of the table, Virginia the other. On either side were Doctor and Mrs. Cockburn; McDonald, the Chief Trader; Richardson, the clerk, and Crane, the missionary of the Church of England. Matthews served with rigid precision in the order of importance, first the Factor, then Virginia, then the doctor, his wife, McDonald, the clerk, and Crane in due order. On entering a room the same precedence would have held good. Thus these people, six hundred miles as the crow flies from the nearest settlement, maintained their shadowy hold on civilization.

The glass was fine, the silver massive, the linen dainty, Matthews waited faultlessly: but overhead hung the rough timbers of the wilderness post, across the river faintly could be heard the howling of wolves. The fare was rice, curry, salt pork, potatoes, and beans; for at this season the game was poor, and the fish hardly yet running with regularity.

Throughout the meal Virginia sat in a singular abstraction. No conscious thoughts took shape in her mind, but nevertheless she seemed to herself to be occupied in considering weighty matters. When directly addressed, she answered sweetly. Much of the time she studied her father's face. She found it old. Those lines were already evident which, when first noted, bring a stab of surprised pain to the breast of a child—the droop of the mouth, the wrinkling of the temples, the patient weariness of the eyes. Virginia's own eyes filled with tears. The subjective passive state into which a newly born but not yet recognized love had cast her, inclined her to gentleness. She accepted facts as they came to her. For the moment she forgot the mere happenings of the day, and lived only in the resulting mood of them all. The new-comer inspired her no longer with anger nor sorrow, attraction nor fear. Her active emotions in abeyance, she floated dreamily on the clouds of a new estate.

This very aloofness of spirit disinclined her for the company of the others after the meal was finished. The Factor closeted himself with Richardson. The doctor, lighting a cheroot, took his way across to his infirmary. McDonald, Crane, and Mrs. Cockburn entered the drawing-room and seated themselves near the piano. Virginia hesitated, then threw a shawl over her head and stepped out on the broad veranda.

At once the vast, splendid beauty of the Northern night broke over her soul. Straight before her gleamed and flashed and ebbed and palpitated the aurora. One moment its long arms shot beyond the zenith; the next it had broken and rippled back like a brook of light to its arch over the Great Bear. Never for an instant was it still. Its restlessness stole away the quiet of the evening; but left it magnificent.

In comparison with this coruscating dome of the infinite the earth had shrunken to a narrow black band of velvet, in which was nothing distinguishable until suddenly the sky-line broke in calm silhouettes of spruce and firs. And always the mighty River of the Moose, gleaming, jewelled, barbaric in its reflections, slipped by to the sea.

So rapid and bewildering was the motion of these two great powers—the river and the sky—that the imagination could not believe in silence. It was as though the earth were full of shoutings and of tumults. And yet in reality the night was as still as a tropical evening. The wolves and the sledge-dogs answered each other undisturbed; the beautiful songs of the white-throats stole from the forest as divinely instinct as ever with the spirit of peace.

Virginia leaned against the railing and looked upon it all. Her heart was big with emotions, many of which she could not name;

her eyes were full of tears. Something had changed in her since yesterday, but she did not know what it was. The faint wise stars, the pale moon just sinking, the gentle south breeze could have told her, for they are old, old in the world's affairs. Occasionally a flash more than ordinarily brilliant would glint one of the bronze guns beneath the flag-staff. Then Virginia's heart would glint too. She imagined the reflection startled her.

She stretched her arms out to the night, embracing its glories, sighing in sympathy with its meaning, which she did not know. She felt the desire of restlessness; yet she could not bear to go. But no thought of the stranger touched her, for you see as yet she did not understand.

Then, quite naturally, she heard his voice in the darkness close to her knee. It seemed inevitable that he should be there; part of the restless, glorious night, part of her mood. She gave no start of surprise, but half closed her eyes and leaned her fair head against a pillar of the veranda. He sang in a sweet undertone an old *chanson* of voyage.

> *"Par derrièr' chez mon père,*
> *Vole, mon coeur, vole!*
> *Par derrièr' chez mon père*
> *Li-ya-t-un pommier doux."*

"Ah lady, lady mine," broke in the voice softly, "the night too is sweet, soft as thine eyes. Will you not greet me?"

The girl made no sign. After a moment the song went on.

> *"Trois filles d'un prince,*
> *Vole, mon coeur, vole!*
> *Trois filles d'un prince*
> *Sont endormies dessous."*

"Will not the princess leave her sisters of dreams?" whispered the voice, fantastically. "Will she not come?"

Virginia shivered, and half-opened her eyes, but did not stir. It seemed that the darkness sighed, then became musical again.

> *"La plus jeun' se réveille,*
> *Vole, mon coeur, vole!*

La plus jeun' se réveille
—Ma Soeur, voilà le jour!"

The song broke this time without a word of pleading. The girl opened her eyes wide and stared breathlessly straight before her at the singer.

"—Non, ce n'est qu'une étoile,
Vole, mon coeur, vole!
Non, ce n'est qu'une étoile
Qu'éclaire nos amours!"

The last word rolled out through its passionate throat tones and died into silence.

"Come!" repeated the man again, this time almost in the accents of command.

She turned slowly and went to him, her eyes childlike and frightened, her lips wide, her face pale. When she stood face to face with him she swayed and almost fell.

"What do you want with me?" she faltered, with a little sob.

The man looked at her keenly, laughed, and exclaimed in an every-day, matter-of-fact voice:

"Why, I really believe my song frightened you. It is only a boating song. Come, let us go and sit on the gun-carriages and talk."

"Oh!" she gasped, a trifle hysterically. "Don't do that again Please don't. I do not understand it! You must not!"

He laughed again, but with a note of tenderness in his voice, and took her hand to lead her away, humming in an undertone the last couplet of his song:

"Non, ce n'est qu'une étoile,
Qu'éclaire nos amours!"

CHAPTER EIGHT

Virginia went with this man passively—to an appointment which, but an hour ago, she had promised herself she would not keep. Her inmost soul was stirred, just before. Then it had been few words, now it was a little common song. But the strange power of the man held her close, so she realized that for the moment at least she would do as he desired. In the amazement and consternation of this thought she found time to offer up a little prayer: "Dear God, make him kind to me."

They leaned against the old bronze guns, facing the river. He pulled her shawl about her, masterfully yet with gentleness, and then, as though it was the most natural thing in the world, he drew her to him until she rested against his shoulder. And she remained there, trembling, in suspense, glancing at him quickly, in birdlike, pleading glances, as though praying him to be kind. He took no notice after that, so the act seemed less like a caress than a matter of course. He began to talk, half-humorously, and little by little, as he went on, she forgot her fears, even her feeling of strangeness, and fell completely under the spell of his power.

"My name is Ned Trent," he told her, "and I am from Quebec. I am a woods runner. I have journeyed far. I have been to the uttermost ends of the North, even up beyond the Hills of Silence."

And then, in his gay, half-mocking, yet musical voice he touched lightly on vast and distant things. He talked of the great Saskatchewan, of Peace River, and the delta of the Mackenzie, of the winter journeys beyond Great Bear Lake into the Land of the Little Sticks, and the half-mythical lake of Yamba Tooh. He spoke of life with the Dog Ribs and Yellow Knives, where the snow falls in midsummer. Before her eyes slowly spread, like a panorama, the whole extent of the great North, with its fierce, hardy men, its dreadful journeys by canoe and sledge, its frozen barrens, its mighty forests, its solemn charm. All at once this post of Conjuror's House, a month in the wilderness as it was, seemed very small and tame and civilized for the simple reason that Death did not always compass it about.

"It was very cold then," said Ned Trent, "and very hard. *Le grand frête* of winter had come. At night we had no other shelter than our blankets, and we could not keep a fire because the spruce burned too fast and threw too many coals. For a long time we shivered, curled up on our snow-shoes; then fell heavily asleep, so that even the dogs fighting over us did not awaken us. Two or three times in the night we boiled tea. We had to thaw our moccasins each morning by thrusting them inside our shirts. Even the Indians were shivering and saying, 'Ed-sa, yazzi ed-sa'—'it is cold, very cold.' And when we came to Rae it was not much better. A roaring fire in the fireplace could not prevent the ink from freezing on the pen. This went on for five months."

Thus he spoke, as one who says common things. He said little of himself, but as he went on in short, curt sentences the picture grew more distinct, and to Virginia the man became more and more prominent in it. She saw the dying and exhausted dogs, the frost-rimed, weary men; she heard the quick *crunch, crunch, crunch* of the snow-shoes hurrying ahead to break the trail; she felt the cruel torture of the *mal de raquette*, the shrivelling bite of the frost, the pain of snow blindness, the hunger that yet could not stomach the frozen fish nor the hairy, black caribou meat. One thing she could not conceive—the indomitable spirit of the men. She glanced timidly up at her companion's face.

"The Company is a cruel master," she sighed at last, standing upright, then leaning against the carriage of the gun. He let her go without protest, almost without thought, it seemed.

"But not mine," said he.

She exclaimed, in astonishment, "Are you not of the Company?"

"I am no man's man but my own," he answered, simply.

"Then why do you stay in this dreadful North?" she asked.

"Because I love it. It is my life. I want to go where no man has set foot before me; I want to stand alone under the sky; I want to show myself that nothing is too big for me—no difficulty, no hardship—nothing!"

"Why did you come here, then? Here at least are forests so that you can keep warm. This is not so dreadful as the Coppermine, and the country of the Yellow Knives. Did you come here to try *la Longue Traverse* of which you spoke today?"

He fell suddenly sombre, biting in reflection at his lip.

"No—yes—why not?" he said, at length.

"I know you will come out of it safely," said she; "I feel it. You are brave and used to travel. Won't you tell me about it?"

He did not reply. After a moment she looked up in surprise. His brows were knit in reflection. He turned to her again, his eyes glowing into hers. Once more the fascination of the man grew big, overwhelmed her. She felt her heart flutter, her consciousness swim, her old terror returning.

"Listen," said he. "I may come to you tomorrow and ask you to choose between your divine pity and what you might think to be your duty. Then I will tell you all there is to know of *la Longue Traverse*. Now it is a secret of the Company. You are a Factor's daughter; you know what that means." He dropped his head. "Ah, I am tired—tired with it all!" he cried, in a voice strangely unhappy. "But yesterday I played the game with all my old spirit; today the zest is gone! I no longer care." He felt the pressure of her hand. "Are you just a little sorry for me?" he asked. "Sorry for a weakness you do not understand? You must think me a fool."

"I know you are unhappy," replied Virginia, gently. "I am truly sorry for that."

"Are you? Are you, indeed?" he cried. "Unhappiness is worth such pity as yours." He brooded for a moment, then threw his hands out with what might have been a gesture of desperate indifference. Suddenly his mood changed in the whimsical, bewildering fashion of the man. "Ah, a star shoots!" he exclaimed, gayly. "That means a kiss!"

Still laughing, he attempted to draw her to him. Angry, mortified, outraged, she fought herself free and leaped to her feet.

"Oh!" she cried, in insulted anger.

"Oh!" she cried, in a red shame.

"Oh!" she cried, in sorrow.

Her calm broke. She burst into the violent sobbing of a child, and turned and ran hurriedly to the factory.

Ned Trent stared after her a minute from beneath scowling brows. He stamped his moccasined foot impatiently.

"Like a rat in a trap!" he jeered at himself. "Like a rat in a trap, Ned Trent! The fates are drawing around you close. You need just one little thing, and you cannot get it. Bribery is useless! Force is useless! Craft is useless! This afternoon I thought I saw another way. What I could get no other way I might get from this little girl. She is only a child. I believe I could touch her pity—ah, Ned Trent. Ned Trent, can you ever forget her frightened, white face begging you to be kind?" He paced back and forth between the two bronze guns with long, straight strides, like a panther in a cage. "Her aid is mine for the asking—but she makes it impossible to ask! I could not do it. Better try *la Longue Traverse* than take advantage of her pity—she'd surely get into trouble. What wonderful eyes she has. She thinks I am a brute—how she sobbed, as though her little heart had broken. Well, it was the only way to destroy her interest in me. I had to do it. Now she will despise me and forget me. It is better that she should think me a brute than that I should be always haunted by those pleading eyes." The door of the distant church house opened and closed. He smiled bitterly. "To be sure, I haven't tried that," he acknowledged. "Their teachings are singularly apropos to my case—mercy, justice, humanity—yes, and love of man. I'll try it. I'll call for help on the love of man, since I cannot on the love of woman. The love of woman—ah—yes."

He set his feet reflectively toward the chapel.

CHAPTER NINE

After a moment he pushed open the door without ceremony, and entered. He bent his brows, studying the Reverend Archibald Crane, while the latter, looking up startled, turned pink.

He was a pink little man, anyway, the Reverend Archibald Crane, and why, in the inscrutability of its wisdom, the Church had sent him out to influence strong, grim men, the Church in its inscrutable wisdom only knows. He wore at the moment a cambric English boating-hat to protect his bald head from the draught, a full clerical costume as far as the trousers, which were of lavender, and a pair of beaded moccasins faced with red. His weak little face was pink, and two tufts of side-whiskers were nearly so. A heavy gold-headed cane stood at his hand. When he heard the door open he exclaimed, before raising his head, "My, these first flies of the season do bother me so!" and then looked startled.

"Good-evening," greeted Ned Trent, stopping squarely in the centre of the room.

The clergyman spread his arms along the desk's edge in embarrassment.

"Good-evening," he returned, reluctantly. "Is there anything I can do for you?" The visitor puzzled him, but was dressed as a *voyageur*. The Reverend Archibald immediately resolved to treat him as such.

"I wish to introduce myself as Ned Trent," went on the Free Trader with composure, "and I have broken in on your privacy this evening only because I need your ministrations cruelly."

"I am rejoiced that in your difficulties you turn to the consolations of the Church," replied the other in the cordial tones of the man who is always ready. "Pray be seated. He whose soul thirsteth need offer no apology to the keeper of the spiritual fountains."

"Quite so," replied the stranger dryly, seating himself as suggested, "only in this case my wants are temporal rather than spiritual. They, however, seem to me fully within the province of the Church."

"The Church attempts within limits to aid those who are materially in want," assured Crane, with official dignity. "Our resources are small, but to the truly deserving we are always ready to give in the spirit of true giving."

"I am rejoiced to hear it," returned the young man, grimly; "you will then have no difficulty in getting me so small a matter as a rifle and about forty or fifty rounds of ammunition."

A pause of astonishment ensued.

"Why, really," ejaculated Crane, "I fail to see how that falls within my jurisdiction in the slightest. You should see our Trader, or. McDonald, in regard to all such things. Your request addressed to me becomes extraordinary."

"Not so much so when you know who I am. I told you my name is Ned Trent, but I neglected to inform you further that I am a captured Free Trader, condemned to *la Longue Traverse*, and that I have in vain tried to procure elsewhere the means of escape."

Then the clergyman understood. The full significance of the intruder's presence flashed over his little pink face in a trouble of uneasiness. The probable consequences of such a bit of charity as his visitor proposed almost turned him sick with excitement.

"You expect to have them of me!" he cried, getting his voice at last.

"Certainly," assured his interlocutor, crossing his legs comfortably. "Don't you see the logic of events forces me to think so? What other course is open to you? I am in this country entirely within my legal rights as a citizen of the Canadian Commonwealth. Unjustly, I am seized by a stronger power and condemned unjustly to death. Surely you admit the injustice?"

"Well, of course you know—the customs of the country—it is hardly an abstract question—" stammered Crane, still without grasp on the logic of his argument.

"But as an abstract question the injustice is plain," resumed the Free Trader, imperturbably. "And against plain injustice it strikes me there is but one course open to an acknowledged institution of abstract—and concrete—morality. The Church must set itself against immorality, and you, as the Church's representative, must get me a rifle."

"You forget one thing," rejoined Crane.

"What is that?"

"Such an aid would be a direct act of rebellion against authority on my part, which would be severely punished. Of course," he asserted, with conscious righteousness, "I should not consider that for a moment as far as my own personal safety is concerned. But my cause would suffer. You forget, sir, that we are doing here a great and good work. We have in our weekly congregational singing over forty regular attendants from the aborigines; next year I hope to build a church at Whale River, thus reaching the benighted inhabitants of that distant region. All of this is a vital matter in the service of our Lord and Saviour Jesus Christ. You suggest that I endanger all this in order to right a single instance of injustice. Of course we are told to love one another, but—" he paused.

"You have to compromise," finished the stranger for him.

"Exactly," said the Reverend Crane. "Thank you; it is exactly that. In order to accomplish what little good the Lord vouchsafes to our poor efforts, we are obliged to overlook many things. Otherwise we should not be allowed to stay here at all."

"That is most interesting," agreed Ned Trent, with a rather biting calm. "But is it not a little calculating? My slight familiarity with religious history and literature has always led me to believe that you are taught to embrace the right at any cost whatsoever—that, if you give yourself unreservedly to justice, the Lord will sustain you through all trials. I think at a pinch I could even quote a text to that effect."

"My dear fellow," objected the Reverend Archibald in gentle protest, "you evidently do not understand the situation at all. I feel I should be most untrue to my trust if I were to endanger in any way the life-long labor of my predecessor. You must be able to see that for yourself. It would destroy utterly my usefulness here. They'd send me away. I couldn't go on with the work. I have to think what is for the best."

"There is some justice in what you say," admitted the stranger, "if you persist in looking on this thing as a business proposition. But it seems to my confessedly untrained mind that you missed the point. 'Trust in the Lord,' saith the prophet. In fact, certain rivals in your own field hold the doctrine you expound, and you consider them wrong. 'To do evil that good may come' I seem to recognize as a tenet of the Church of the Jesuits."

"I protest. I really do protest," objected the clergyman, scandalized.

"All right," agreed Ned Trent, with good-natured contempt. "That is not the point. Do you refuse?"

"Can't you see?" begged the other. "I'm sure you are reasonable enough to take the case on its broader side."

"You refuse?" insisted Ned Trent.

"It is not always easy to walk straightly before the Lord, and my way is not always clear before me, but—"

"You refuse!" cried Ned Trent, rising impatiently.

The Reverend Archibald Crane looked at his catechiser with a trace of alarm.

"I'm sorry; I'm afraid I must," he apologized.

The stranger advanced until he touched the desk on the other side of which the Reverend Archibald was sitting, where he stood for some moments looking down on his opponent with an almost amused expression of contempt.

"You are an interesting little beast," he drawled, "and I've seen a lot of your kind in my time. Here you preach every Sunday, to whomever will listen to you, certain cut-and-dried doctrines you don't believe practically in the least. Here for the first time you have had a chance to apply them literally, and you hide behind a lot of words. And while you're about it you may as well hear what I have to say about your kind. I've had a pretty wide experience in the North, and I know what I'm talking about. Your work here among the Indians is rot, and every sensible man knows it. You coop them up in your log-built houses, you force on them clothes to which they are unaccustomed until they die of consumption. Under your little tin-steepled imitation of civilization, for which they are not fitted, they learn to beg, to steal, to lie. I have travelled far, but I have yet to discover what your kind are allowed on earth for. You are narrow-minded, bigoted, intolerant, and without a scrap of real humanity to ornament your mock religion. When you find you can't meddle with other people's affairs enough at home you get sent where you can get right in the business—and earn salvation for doing it. I don't know just why I should say this to you, but it sort of does me good to tell it. Once I heard one of your kind tell a sorrowing mother that her little child had gone to hell because it had died before he—the smug hypocrite—had sprinkled its little body with a handful of water. There's humanity for you! It may interest you to know that I thrashed that man then and there. You are all alike; I know the breed. When there is found a real man among you—and there are such—he is so different in everything, including his religion, as to be really of another race. I came here without the slightest expectation of getting what I asked for. As I said before, I know your breed, and I know just how well your two-thousand-year-old doctrines apply to practical cases. There is another way, but I hated to use it. You'd take it quick enough, I dare say. Here is where I should receive aid. I may have to get it where I should not. You a man of God! Why, you poor little insect, I can't even get angry at you!"

He stood for a moment looking at the confused and troubled clergyman. Then he went out.

CHAPTER TEN

Almost immediately the door opened again.

"You, Miss Albret!" cried Crane.

"What does this mean?" demanded Virginia, imperiously. "Who is that man? In what danger does he stand? What does he want a rifle for? I insist on knowing."

She stood straight and tall in the low room, her eyes flashing, her head thrown back in the assured power of command.

The Reverend Crane tried to temporize, hesitating over his words. She cut him short.

"That is nonsense. Everybody seems to know but myself. I am no child. I came to consult you—my spiritual adviser—in regard to this very case. Accidentally I overheard enough to justify me in knowing more."

The clergyman murmured something about the Company's secrets. Again she cut him short.

"Company's secrets! Since when has the Company confided in Andrew Laviolette, in Wishkobun, in *you*!"

"Possibly you would better ask your father," said Crane, with some return of dignity.

"It does not suit me to do so," replied she. "I insist that you answer my questions. Who is this man?"

"Ned Trent, he says."

"I will not be put off in this way. *Who* is he? *What* is he?"

"He is a Free Trader," replied the Reverend Crane with the air of a man who throws down a bomb and is afraid of the consequences. To his astonishment the bomb did not explode.

"What is that?" she asked, simply.

The man's jaw dropped and his eyes opened in astonishment. Here was a density of ignorance in regard to the ordinary affairs of the Post which could by no stretch of the imagination be ascribed to chance. If Virginia Albret did not know the meaning of the term, and all the tragic consequences it entailed, there could be but one conclusion: Galen Albret had not intended that she should know. She had purposely been left in ignorance, and a politic man would hesitate long before daring to enlighten her. The Reverend Crane, in sheer terror, became sullen.

"A Free Trader is a man who trades in opposition to the Company," said he, cautiously.

"What great danger is he in?" the girl persisted with her catechism.

"None that I am aware of," replied Crane, suavely. "He is a very ill-balanced and excitable young man."

Virginia's quick instincts recognized again the same barrier which, with the people, with Wishkobun, with her father, had shut her so effectively from the truth. Her power of femininity and position had to give way before the man's fear for himself and of Galen Albret's unexpressed wish. She asked a few more questions, received a few more evasive replies, and left the little clergyman to recover as best he might from a very trying evening.

Out in the night the girl hesitated in two minds as to what to do next. She was excited, and resolved to finish the affair, but she could not bring her courage to the point of questioning her father. That the stranger was in antagonism to the Company, that he believed himself to be in danger on that account, that he wanted succor, she saw clearly enough. But the whole affair was vague, disquieting. She wanted to see it plainly, know its reasons. And beneath her excitement she recognized, with a catch of the breath, that she was afraid for him. She had not time now to ask herself what it might mean; she only realized the presence of the fact.

She turned instinctively in the direction of Doctor Cockburn's house. Mrs. Cockburn was a plain little middle-aged woman with parted gray hair and sweet, faded eyes. In the life of the place she was a nonentity, and her tastes were homely and commonplace, but Virginia liked her.

She proved to be at home, the Doctor still at his dispensary, which was well. Virginia entered a small log room, passed through it immediately to a larger papered room, and sat down in a musty red arm-chair. The building was one of the old régime, which meant that its floor was of wide and rather uneven painted boards, its ceiling low, its windows small, and its general lines of an irregular and sagging rule-of-thumb tendency. The white wall-paper evidently concealed squared logs. The present inhabitants, being possessed at once of rather homely tastes and limited facilities, had over-furnished the place with an infinitude of little things—

little rugs, little tables, little knit doilies, little racks of photographs, little china ornaments, little spidery what-nots, and shelves for books.

Virginia seated herself, and went directly to the topic.

"Mrs. Cockburn," she said, "you have always been very good to me, always, ever since I came here as a little girl. I have not always appreciated it, I am afraid, but I am in great trouble, and I want your help."

"What is it, dearie," asked the older woman, softly. "Of course I will do anything I can."

"I want you to tell me what all this mystery is—about the man who today arrived from Kettle Portage, I mean. I have asked everybody: I have tried by all means in my power to get somebody somewhere to tell me. It is maddening—and I have a special reason for wanting to know."

The older woman was already gazing at her through troubled eyes.

"It is a shame and a mistake to keep you so in ignorance!" she broke out, "and I have said so always. There are many things you have the right to know, although some of them would make you very unhappy—as they do all of us poor women who have to live in this land of dread. But in this I cannot, dearie."

Virginia felt again the impalpable shadow of truth escaping her. Baffled, confused, she began to lose her self-control. A dozen times today she had reached after this thing, and always her fingers had closed on empty air. She felt that she could not stand the suspense of bewilderment a single instant longer. The tears overflowed and rolled down her cheeks unheeded.

"Oh, Mrs. Cockburn!" she cried. "Please! You do not know how dreadful this thing has come to be to me just because it is made so mysterious. Why has it been kept from me alone? It must have something to do with me, and I can't stand this mystery, this double-dealing, another minute. If you won't tell me, nobody will. and I shall go on imagining—Oh, please have pity on me! I feel the shadow of a tragedy. It comes out in everything, in everybody to whom I turn. I see it in Wishkobun's avoidance of me, in my father's silence, in Mr. Crane's confusion, in your reluctance—yes, in the very reckless insolence of Mr. Trent himself!"—

her voice broke slightly. "If you will not tell me, I shall go direct to my father," she ended, with more firmness.

Mrs. Cockburn examined the girl's flushed face through kindly but shrewd and experienced eyes. Then, with a caressing little murmur of pity, she arose and seated herself on the arm of the red chair, taking the girl's hand in hers.

"I believe you mean it," she said, "and I am going to tell you myself. There is much sorrow in it for you; but if you go to your father it will only make it worse. I am doing what I should not. It is shameful that such things happen in this nineteenth century, but happen they do. The long and short of it is that the Factors of this Post tolerate no competition in the country, and when a man enters it for the purpose of trading with the Indians, he is stopped and sent out."

"There is nothing very bad about that," said Virginia, relieved.

"No, my dear, not in that. But they say his arms and supplies are taken from him, and he is given a bare handful of provisions. He has to make a quick journey, and to starve at that. Once when I was visiting out at the front, not many years ago, I saw one of those men—they called him Jo Bagneau—and his condition was pitiable—pitiable!"

"But hardships can be endured. A man can escape."

"Yes," almost whispered Mrs. Cockburn, looking about her apprehensively, "but the story goes that there are some cases—when the man is an old offender, or especially determined, or so prominent as to be able to interest the law—no one breathes of these cases here—but—*he never gets out!*"

"What do you mean?" cried Virginia, harshly.

"One dares not mean such things; but they are so. The hardships of the wilderness are many, the dangers terrible—what more natural than that a man should die of them in the forest? It is no one's fault."

"What do you mean?" repeated Virginia; "for God's sake speak plainly!"

"I dare not speak plainer than I know; and no one ever really *knows* anything about it—excepting the Indian who fires the shot, or who watches the man until he dies of starvation," whispered Mrs. Cockburn.

"But—but!" cried the girl, grasping her companion's arm "My father! Does *he* give such orders? *He?*"

"No orders are given. The thing is understood. Certain runners, whose turn it is, shadow the Free Trader. Your father is not responsible; no one is responsible. It is the policy."

"And this man—"

"It has gone about that he is to take *la Longue Traverse*. He knows it himself."

"It is barbaric, horrible; it is murder."

"My dear, it is all that; but this is the country of dread. You have known the soft, bright side always—the picturesque men, the laugh, the song. If you had seen as much of the harshness of wilderness life as a doctor's wife must you would know that when the storms of their great passions rage it is well to sit quiet at your prayers."

The girl's eyes were wide-fixed, staring at this first reality of life. A thousand new thoughts jostled for recognition. Suddenly her world had been swept from beneath her. The ancient patriarchal, kindly rule had passed away, and in its place she was forced to see a grim iron bond of death laid over her domain. And her father—no longer the grave, kindly old man—had become the ruthless tyrant. All these bright, laughing *voyageurs*, playmates of her childhood, were in reality executioners of a savage blood-law. She could not adjust herself to it.

She got to her feet with an effort.

"Thank you, Mrs. Cockburn," she said, in a low voice. "I—I do not quite understand. But I must go now. I must—I must see that my father's room is ready for him," she finished, with the proud defensive instinct of the woman who has been deeply touched. "You know I always do that myself."

"Good-night, dearie," replied the older woman, understanding well the girl's desire to shelter behind the commonplace. She leaned forward and kissed her. "God keep and guide you. I hope I have done right."

"Yes," cried Virginia, with unexpected fire. "Yes, you did just right! I ought to have been told long ago! They've kept me a perfect child to whom everything has been bright and care-free and simple. I—I feel that until this moment I have lacked my real womanhood!"

She bowed her head and passed through the log room into the outer air.

Her father, *her* father, had willed this man's death, and so he was to die! That explained many things—the young fellow's insolence, his care-free recklessness, his passionate denunciation of the Reverend Crane and the Reverend Crane's religion. He wanted one little thing—the gift of a rifle wherewith to assure his subsistence should he escape into the forest—and of all those at Conjuror's House to whom he might turn for help, some were too hard to give it to him, and some too afraid! He should have it! She, the daughter of her father, would see to it that in this one instance her father's sin should fail! Suddenly, in the white heat of her emotion, she realized why these matters stirred her so profoundly, and she stopped short and gasped with the shock of it. It did not matter that she thwarted her father's will; it would not matter if she should be discovered and punished as only these harsh characters could punish. For the brave bearing, the brave jest, the jaunty facing of death, the tender, low voice, the gay song, the aurora-lit moment of his summons—all these had at last their triumph. She knew that she loved him; and that if he were to die, she would surely die too.

And, oh, it must be that he loved her! Had she not heard it in the music of his voice from the first?—the passion of his tones? the dreamy, lyrical swing of his talk by the old bronze guns?

Then she staggered sharply, and choked back a cry. For out of her recollections leaped two sentences of his—the first careless, imprudent, unforgivable; the second pregnant with meaning. "*Ah, a star shoots!*" he had said. "*That means a kiss!*" and again, to the clergyman, "*I came here without the slightest expectation of getting what I asked for. There is another way, but I hate to use it.*"

She was the other way! She saw it plainly. He did not love her, but he saw that he could fascinate her, and he hoped to use her as an aid to his escape. She threw her head up proudly.

Then a man swung into view across the Northern Lights. Virginia pressed back against the palings among the bushes until he should have passed. It was Ned Trent, returning from a walk to the end of the island. He was alone and unfollowed, and the girl realized with a sudden grip at the heart that the wilderness itself was sufficient safe-guard against a man unarmed and unequipped. It was not considered worth while even to watch him. Should he escape, unarmed as he was, sure death by starvation awaited him in the land of dread.

As he entered the settlement he struck up an air.

> "Le fils du roi s'en va chassant,
> En roulant ma boule,
> Avec son grand fusil d'argent,
> Rouli roulant, ma boule roulant."

Almost immediately a window slid back, and an exasperated voice cried out:

"*Hólà* dere, w'at one time dam fool you for mak' de sing so late!"

The voice went on imperturbably:

> "Avec son grand fusil d'argent,
> En roulant ma boule,
> Visa le noir, tua le blanc,
> Rouli roulant, ma boule roulant."

"*Sacrè!*" shrieked the habitant.

"Hello, Johnny Frenchman!" called Ned Trent, in his acid tones. "That you? Be more polite, or I'll stand here and sing you the whole of it."

The window slammed shut.

Ned Trent took up his walk again toward some designated sleeping-place of his own, his song dying into the distance.

> "Visa le noir, tua le blanc,
> En roulant ma boule,
> O fils du roi, tu es méchant!
> Rouli roulant, ma boule roulant."

"And he can *sing!*" cried the girl bitterly to herself. "At such a time! Oh, my dear God, help me, help me! I am the unhappiest girl alive!"

CHAPTER ELEVEN

Virginia did not sleep at all that night. She was reaching toward her new self. Heretofore she had ruled those about her proudly, secure in her power and influence. Now she saw that all along her influence had in not one jot exceeded that of the winsome girl. She had no real power at all. They went mercilessly on in the grim way of their fathers, dealing justice even-handed according to their own crude conceptions of it, without thought of God or man. She turned hot all over as she saw herself in this new light—as she saw those about her indulgently smiling at her airs of the mistress of it. It angered her—though the smile might be good-humored, even affectionate.

And she shrank into herself with utter loathing when she remembered Ned Trent. There indeed her woman's pride was hard stricken. She recalled with burning cheeks how his intense voice had stirred her; how his wishes had compelled her; she shivered pitifully as she remembered the warmth of his shoulder touching carelessly her own. If he had come to her honestly and asked her aid, she would have given it; but this underhand pretence at love! It was unworthy of him; and it was certainly most unworthy of her. What must he think of her? How he must be laughing at her—and hoping that his spell was working, so that he could get the coveted rifle and the forty cartridges.

"I hate him!" she cried to herself, the backs of her long, slender hands pressed against her eyes. She meant that she loved him, but for the purposes in hand one would do as well as the other.

At earliest daylight she was up. Bathing her face and throat in cold water, and hastily catching her beautiful light hair under a cap, she slipped down stairs and out past the stockade to the point. There she seated herself, a heavy shawl about her, and gave herself up to reflection. She had approached silently, her moccasins giving no sound. Presently she became aware that someone was there before her. Looking toward the river she saw on the next level below her a man, seated on a bowlder, and gazing to the south.

His very soul was in his eyes. Virginia gasped at the change in him since last she had seen him. The gay, mocking demeanor which had seemed an essential part of his very flesh and blood had fallen away from him, leaving a sad and lofty dignity that ennobled his countenance. The lines of his face were stern, of his mouth pathetic; his eyes yearned. He stared toward the south with an almost mesmeric intensity, as though he hoped by sheer longing to materialize a vision. Tears sprang to the girl's eyes at the subtle pathos of his attitude.

He stretched his arms wearily over his head, and sighed deeply and looked up. His eyes rested on the girl without surprise; the expression of his features did not change.

"Pardon me," he said, simply. "Today is my last of plenty. I am up enjoying it."

Virginia had anticipated the usual instantaneous transformation of his manner when he should catch sight of her. Her resentment was dispelled. In face of the vaster tragedies little considerations gave way.

"Do you leave—today?" she asked, in a low voice.

"Tomorrow morning, early," he corrected. "Today I found my provisions packed and laid at my door. It is a hint I know how to take."

"You have everything you need?" asked the girl, with an assumption of indifference.

He looked her in the eyes for a moment.

"Everything," he lied, calmly.

Virginia perceived that he lied, and her heart stood still with a sudden hope that perhaps, at this eleventh hour, he might have repented of his unworthy intentions toward herself. She leaned to him over the edge of the little rise.

"Have you a rifle—for *la Longue Traverse*?" she inquired, with meaning.

He stared at her a little the harder.

"Why—why, surely," he replied, in a tone less confident. "Nobody travels without a rifle in the North."

She dropped swiftly down the slope and stood face to face with him.

"Listen," she began, in her superb manner. "I know all there is to know. You are a Free Trader, and you are to be sent to your death. It is murder, and it is done by my father." She held her head proudly, but the notes of her voice were straining. "I knew nothing of this yesterday. I was a foolish girl who thought all men were good and just, and that all those whom I knew were noble. My eyes are open now. I see injustice being done by my own household, and"—tears were trembling near her lashes, but she blinked them back—"and I am no longer a foolish girl! You need not try to deceive me. You must tell me what I can do, for I cannot permit so great a wrong to be done by my father without attempting to set it right." This was not what she had intended to say, but suddenly the course was clear to her. The influence of the man had again swept over her, drowning her will, filling her with the old fear, which was now for the moment turned to pride by the character of the situation.

But to her surprise the man was thinking of something else.

"Who told you?" he demanded, harshly. Then, without waiting for a reply, "It was that little preacher; I'll have an interview with him!"

"No, no!" protested the girl. "It was not he. It was a friend. I had the right to know."

"You had no right!" he cried, vehemently. "You and life should have nothing to do with each other. There is a look in your eyes that was not in them yesterday, and the one who put it there is not your friend." He stood staring at her intently, as one who ponders what is best to do. Then very quietly he took her hands and drew her to a place beside him on the bowlder.

"I am going to tell you something, little girl," said he, "and you must listen quietly to the end. Perhaps at the last you may see more clearly than you do now.

"This old Company of yours has been established for a great many years. Back in old days, over two centuries ago, it pushed up into this wilderness to trade for its furs. That you know. And then it explored ever farther to the west and the north, until its servants stood on the shores of the Pacific and the stretches of the Arctic Ocean. And its servants loved it. Enduring immense hardships, cut off from their kind, outlining dimly with the eye of faith the structure of a mighty power, they loved it always. Thousands of men were in its employ, and so loyal were they that its secrets were safe and its prestige was defended, often to a lonely death. I have known the Company and its servants for a long time, and if I had leisure I could instance a hundred examples of devotion and sacrifice beside which mere patriotism would seem a little thing. Men who had no country cleaved to her desolate posts, her lakes and rivers and forests; men who had no home ties felt the tug of her wild life at their hearts; men who had no God bowed in awe before her power and grandeur. The Company was a living thing.

"Rivals attempted her supremacy, and were defeated by the steadfastness of the men who received her meagre wages and looked to her as their one ideal. Her explorers were the bravest, her traders the most enterprising and single-minded, her factors and partners the most capable and potent in all the world. No country, no leader, no State ever received half the worship her sons gave her. The fierce Nor'westers, the traders of Montreal, the Company of the X Y, Astor himself, had to give way. For, although they were bold or reckless or crafty or able, they had not the ideal which raises such qualities to invincibility.

"And, little girl, nothing is wrong to men who have such an ideal before them. They see but one thing, and all means are good that help them to assure that one thing. They front the dangers, they overcome the hardships, they crush the rivals. Bloody wars have taken place in these forests, ruthless deeds have been done, but the men who accomplished them held the deeds good. So for two hundred years, aided by the charter from the king, they have made good their undisputed right.

"Then the railroad entered the west. The charter of monopoly ran out. Through the Nipissing, the Athabasca, the Edmonton, came the Free Traders—men who traded independently. These the Company could not control, so it competed—and to its credit its competition has held its own. Even far into the Northwest, where the trails are long, the Free Traders have established their chains of supplies, entering into rivalry with the Company for a barter it has always considered its right. The medicine has been bitter, but the servants of the Company have adjusted themselves to the new conditions, and are holding their own.

"But one region still remains cut off from the outside world by a broad band of unexplored waste. The life here at Hudson's

Bay—although you may not know it—is exactly the same today that it was two hundred years ago. And here the Company makes its stand for a monopoly.

"At first it worked openly. But in the case of Guillaume Sayer, a daring and pugnacious *mètis*, it got into trouble with the law. Since that time it has wrapped itself in secrecy and mystery, carrying on its affairs behind the screen of five hundred miles of forest. Here it has still the power; no man can establish himself here, can even travel here, without its consent, for it controls the food and the Indians. The Free Trader enters, but he does not stay for long. The Company's servants are mindful of their old fanatical ideal. Nothing is ever known, no orders are ever given, but something happens, and the man never ventures again.

"If he is an ordinary *mètis* or Canadian, he emerges from the forest starved, frightened, thankful. If his story is likely to be believed in high places, he never emerges at all. The dangers of wilderness travel are many: he succumbs to them. That is the whole story. Nothing definite is known; no instances can be proved; your father denies the legend and calls it a myth. The Company claims to be ignorant of it, perhaps its greater officers really are, but the legend holds so good that the journey has its name—*la Longue Traverse*.

"But remember this, no man is to blame—unless it is he who of knowledge takes the chances. It is a policy, a growth of centuries, an idea unchangeable to which the long services of many fierce and loyal men have given substance. A Factor cannot change it. If he did, the thing would be outside of nature, something not to be understood.

"I am here. I am to take *la Longue Traverse*. But no man is to blame. If the scheme of the thing is wrong, it has been so from the very beginning, from the time when King Charles set his signature to the charter of unlimited authority. The history of a thousand men gives the tradition power, gives it insistence. It is bigger than any one individual. It is as inevitable as that water should flow down hill."

He had spoken quietly, but very earnestly, still holding her two hands, and she had sat looking at him unblinking from eyes behind which passed many thoughts. When he had finished, a short pause followed, at the end of which she asked unexpectedly,

"Last evening you told me that you might come to me and ask me to choose between my pity and what I might think to be my duty. What are you going to ask of me?"

"Nothing. I spoke idle words."

"Last evening I overheard you demand something of Mr. Crane," she pursued, without commenting on his answer. "When he refused you I heard you say these words, 'Here is where I should have received aid; I may have to get it where I should not.' What was the aid you asked of him? and where else did you expect to get it?"

"The aid was something impossible to accord, and I did not expect to get it elsewhere. I said that in order to induce him to help me."

A wonderful light sprang to the girl's eyes, but still she maintained her level voice.

"You asked him for a rifle with which to escape. You expected to get it of me. Deny it if you can."

Ned Trent looked at her keenly a moment, then dropped his eyes.

"It is true," said he.

"And the pity was to give you this weapon; and the duty was my duty to my father's house."

"It is true," he repeated, dejectedly.

"And you lied to me when you said you had a rifle with which to journey *la Longue Traverse*."

"That too is true," he acknowledged.

When next she spoke her voice was not quite so well controlled.

"Why did you not ask me, as you intended? Why did you tell me these lies?"

The young man hesitated, looked her in the face, turned away, and murmured,

"I could not."

"Why?" persisted the girl. "Why? You must tell me."

"Because," said Ned Trent—"because it could not be done. Every rifle in the place is known. Because you would be found out in this, and I do not know what your punishment might not be."

"You knew this before?" insisted Virginia, stonily.

"Yes."

"Then why did you change your mind?"

"When first I saw you by the gun," began Ned Trent, in a low voice, "I was a desperate man, clutching at the slightest chance. The thought crossed my mind then that I might use you. Then later I saw that I had some influence over you, and I made my plan. But last night—"

"Yes, last night?" urged Virginia, softly.

"Last night I paced the island, and I found out many things. One of them was that I could not."

"Even though this dreadful journey—"

"I would rather take my chances."

Again there was silence between them.

"It was a good lie," then said Virginia, gently—"a noble lie. And what you have told me to comfort me about my father has been nobly said. And I believe you, for I have known the truth about your fate." He shut his lips grimly. "Why—why did you come?" she cried, passionately. "Is the trade so good, are your needs then so great, that you must run these perils?"

"My needs," he replied. "No; I have enough."

"Then why?" she insisted.

"Because that old charter has long since expired, and now this country is as free for me as for the Company," he explained. "We are in a civilized century, and no man has a right to tell me where I shall or shall not go. Does the Company own the Indians and the creatures of the woods?" Something in the tone of his voice brought her eyes steadily to his for a moment.

"Is that all?" she asked at length.

He hesitated, looked away, looked back again.

"No, it is not," he confessed, in a low voice. "It is a thing I do not speak of. My father was a servant of this Company, a good, true servant. No man was more honest, more zealous, more loyal."

"I am sure of it," said Virginia, softly.

"But in some way that he never knew himself he made enemies in high places. The cowards did not meet him man to man, and so he never knew who they were. If he had, he would have killed them. But they worked against him always. He was given hard posts, inadequate supplies, scant help, and then he was held to account for what he could not do. Finally he left the company in disgrace—undeserved disgrace. He became a Free Trader in the days when to become a Free Trader was worse than attacking a grizzly with cubs. In three years he was killed. But when I grew to be a man"—he clenched his teeth—"by God! how I have *prayed* to know who did it." He brooded for a moment, then went on. "Still, I have accomplished something. I have traded in spite of your factors in many districts. One summer I pushed to the Coppermine in the teeth of them, and traded with the Yellow Knives for the robes of the musk-ox. And they knew me and feared my rivalry, these traders of the Company. No district of the far North but has felt the influence of my bartering. The traders of all districts—Fort au Liard, Lapierre's House, Fort Rae, Ile à la Crosse, Portage la Loche, Lac la Biche, Jasper's House, the House of the Touchwood Hills—all these, and many more, have heard of Ned Trent."

"Your father—you knew him well?"

"No, but I remember him—a tall, dark man, with a smile always in his eyes and a laugh on his lips. I was brought up at a school in Winnipeg under a priest. Two or three times in the year my father used to appear for a few days. I remember well the last time I saw him. I was about thirteen years old. 'You are growing to be a man,' said he; 'next year we will go out on the trail.' I never saw him again."

"What happened?"

"Oh, he was just killed," replied Ned Trent, bitterly.

The girl laid her hand on his arm with an appealing little gesture.

"I am so sorry," said she.

"I have no portrait of him," continued the Free Trader, after an instant. "No gift from his hands; nothing at all of his but this."

He showed her an ordinary little silver match-safe such as men use in the North country.

"They brought that to me at the last—the Indians who came to tell my priest the news; and the priest, who was a good man, gave it to me. I have carried it ever since."

Virginia took it reverently. To her it had all the largeness that envelops the symbol of a great passion. After a moment she looked up in surprise.

"Why!" she exclaimed, "this has a name carved on it!"

"Yes," he replied.

"But the name is Graehme Stewart."

"Of course I could not bear my father's name in a country where it was well known," he explained.

"Of course," she agreed. Impulsively she raised her face to his, her eyes shining. "To me all this is very fine," said she.

He smiled a little sadly. "At least you know why I came."

"Yes," she repeated, "I know why you came. But you are in trouble."

"The chances of war."

"And they have defeated you after all."

"I shall start on *la Longue Traverse* singing 'Rouli roulant.' It's a small defeat, that."

"Listen," said she, rapidly. "When I was quite a small girl Mr. McTavish, of Rupert's House, gave me a little rifle. I have never used it, because I do not care to shoot. That rifle has never been counted, and my father has long since forgotten all about it. You must take that, and escape tonight. I will let you have it on one condition—that you give me your solemn promise never to venture into this country again."

"Yes," he agreed, without enthusiasm nor surprise.

She smiled happily at his gloomy face and listless attitude.

"But I do not want to give up the little rifle entirely," she went on, with dainty preciosity, watching him closely. "As I said, it was a present, given to me when I was quite a small girl. You must return it to me at Quebec, in August. Will you promise to do that?"

He wheeled on her swift as light, the eagerness flashing back into his face.

"You are going to Quebec?" he cried.

"My father wishes me to. I have decided to do so. I shall start with the Abítibi *brigade* in July."

He leaped to his feet.

"I promise!" he exulted, "I promise! Tonight, then! Bring the rifle and the cartridges, and some matches, and a little salt. You must take me across the river in a canoe, for I want them to guess at where I strike the woods. I shall cover my trail. And with ten hours' start, let them catch Ned Trent who can!"

She laughed happily.

"Tonight, then. At the south of the island there is a trail, and at the end of the trail a beach—"

"I know!" he cried.

"Meet me there as soon after dark as you can do so without danger."

He threw his hat into the air and caught it, his face boyishly upturned. Again that something, so vaguely familiar, plucked at her with its ghostly, appealing fingers. She turned swiftly, and seized them, and so found herself in possession of a memory out of her far-off childhood.

"I know you!" she cried. "I have seen you before this!"

He bent his puzzled gaze upon her.

"I was a very little girl," she explained, "and you but a lad. It was at a party, I think, a great and brilliant party, for I remember many beautiful women and fine men. You held me up in your arms for people to see, because I was going on a long journey."

"I remember, of course I do!" he exclaimed.

A bell clanged, turning over and over, calling the Company's men to their day.

"Farewell," she said, hurriedly. "Tonight."

"Tonight," he repeated.

She glided rapidly through the grass, noiseless in her moccasined feet. And as she went she heard his voice humming soft and low,

"Isabeau s'y promène
Le long de son jardin,
Le long de son jardin,
Sur le bord de l'île,
Le long de son jardin."

"How could he *help* singing," murmured Virginia, fondly. "Ah, dear Heaven, but I am the happiest girl alive!"

Such a difference can one night bring about.

CHAPTER TWELVE

The day rose and flooded the land with its fuller life. All through the settlement the Post Indians and half-breeds set about their tasks. Some aided Sarnier with his calking of the bateaux; some worked in the fields; some mended or constructed in the different shops. At eight o'clock the bell rang again, and they ate breakfast. Then a group of seven, armed with muzzle-loading "trade-guns" bound in brass, set out for the marshes in hopes of geese. For the flight was arriving, and the Hudson Bay man knows very well the flavor of goose-flesh, smoked, salted, and barrelled.

Now the *voyageurs* began to stroll into the sun. They were men of leisure. Picturesque, handsome, careless, debonair, they wandered back and forth, smoking their cigarettes, exhibiting their finery. Indian women, wrinkled and careworn, plodded patiently about on various businesses. Indian girls, full of fun and mischief, drifted here and there in arm-locked groups of a dozen, smiling, whispering among themselves, ready to collapse toward a common centre of giggles if addressed by one of the numerous woods-dandies, Indian men stalked singly, indifferent, stolid. Indian children of all sizes and degrees of nakedness darted back and forth, playing strange games. The sound of many voices rose across the air.

Once the voices moderated, when McDonald, the Chief Trader, walked rapidly from the barracks building to the trading store; once they died entirely into a hush of respect, when Galen Albret himself appeared on the broad veranda of the factory. He stood for a moment—hulked broad and black against the white-wash—his hands clasped behind him, gazing abstractedly toward the distant bay. Then he turned into the house to some mysterious and weighty business of his own. The hubbub at once broke out again.

Now about the mouth of the long picketed lane leading to the massive trading store gathered a silent group, bearing packs. These were Indians from the more immediate vicinity, desirous of trading their skins. After a moment McDonald appeared in the doorway, a hundred feet away, and raised his hand. Two of the savages, and two only, trotted down the narrow picket lane, their packs on their shoulders.

McDonald ushered them into a big square room, where the bales were undone and spread abroad. Deftly, silently the Trader sorted the furs, placing to one side or the other the "primes," "seconds," and "thirds" of each species. For a moment he calculated. Then he stepped to a post whereon hung long strings of pierced wooden counters, worn smooth by use. Swiftly he told the strings over. To one of the Indians he gave one with these words:

"Mu-hi-kun, my brother, here be pelts to the value of two hundred 'beaver.' Behold a string, then, of two hundred 'castors,' and in addition I give my brother one fathom of tobacco."

The Indian calculated rapidly, his eye abstracted. He had known exactly the value of his catch, and what he would receive for it in "castors," but had hoped for a larger "present," by which the premium on the standard price is measured.

"Ah hah," he exclaimed, finally, and stepped to one side.

"Sak-we-su, my brother," went on McDonald, "here be pelts to the value of three hundred 'beaver.' Behold a string, then, of three hundred 'castors,' and because you have brought so fine a skin of the otter, behold also a fathom of tobacco and a half sack of flour."

"Good!" ejaculated the Indian.

The Trader then led them to stairs, up which they clambered to where Davis, the Assistant Trader, kept store. There, barred by a heavy wooden grill from the airy loft filled with bright calicoes, sashes, pails, guns, blankets, clothes, and other ornamental and useful things, Sak-we-su and Mu-hi-kun made their choice, trading in the worn wooden "castors" on the string. So much flour, so much tea, so much sugar and powder and lead, so much in clothing. Thus were their simple needs supplied for the year to come. Then the remainder they squandered on all sorts of useless things—beads, silks, sashes, bright handkerchiefs, mirrors. And when the last wooden "castor" was in they went down stairs and out the picket lane, carrying their lighter purchases, but leaving the larger as "debt," to be called for when needed. Two of their companions mounted the stairs as they descended; and two more passed them in the narrow picket lane. So the trade went on.

At once Sak-we-su and Mu-hi-kun were surrounded. In

detail they told what they had done. Then in greater detail their friends told what *they* would have done, until after five minutes of bewildering advice the disconsolate pair would have been only too glad to have exchanged everything—if that had been allowed.

Now the bell rang again. It was "smoke time." Everyone quit work for a half-hour. The sun climbed higher in the heavens. The laughing crews of idlers sprawled in the warmth, gambling, telling stories, singing. Then one might have heard all the picturesque songs of the Far North—"A la claire Fontaine"; "Ma Boule Roulant"; "Par derrièr' chez-mon Père"; "Isabeau s'y promène"; "P'tite Jeanneton"; "Luron, Lurette"; "Chante, Rossignol, chante"; the ever-popular "Malbrouck"; "C'est la belle Françoise"; "Alouette"; or the beautiful and tender "La Violette Dandine." They had good voices, these *voyageurs*, with the French artistic instinct, and it was fine to hear them.

At noon the squaws set out to gather canoe gum on the mainland. They sat huddled in the bottom of their old and leaky canoe, reaching far over the sides to dip their paddles, irregularly placed, silent, mysterious. They did not paddle with the unison of the men, but each jabbed a little short stroke as the time suited her, so that always some paddles were rising and some falling. Into the distance thus they flapped like wounded birds; then rounded a bend, and were gone.

The sun swung over and down the slope. Dinner time had passed; "smoke time" had come again. Squaws brought the first white-fish of the season to the kitchen door of the factory, and Matthews raised the hand of horror at the price they asked. Finally he bought six of about three pounds each, giving in exchange tea to the approximate value of twelve cents. The Indian women went away, secretly pleased over their bargain.

Down by the Indian camp suddenly broke the roar of a dog-fight. Two of the sledge *giddés* had come to teeth, and the friends of both were assisting the cause. The idlers went to see, laughing, shouting, running impromptu races. They sat on their haunches and cheered ironically, and made small bets, and encouraged the frantic old squaw hags who, at imminent risk, were trying to disintegrate the snarling, rolling mass. Over in the high log stockade wherein the Company's sledge animals were confined, other wolf-dogs howled mournfully, desolated at missing the fun.

And always the sun swung lower and lower toward the west, until finally the long northern twilight fell, and the girl in the little white bedroom at the factory bathed her face and whispered for the hundredth time to her beating heart:

"Night has come!"

CHAPTER THIRTEEN

That evening at dinner Virginia studied her father's face again. She saw the square settled line of the jaw under the beard, the unwavering frown of the heavy eyebrows, the unblinking purpose of the cavernous, mysterious eyes. Never had she felt herself very close to this silent, inscrutable man, even in his moments of more affectionate expansion. Now a gulf divided them.

And yet, strangely enough, she experienced no revulsion, no horror, no recoil even. He had merely become more aloof, more incomprehensible; his purposes vaster, less susceptible to the grasp of such as she. There may have been some basis for this feeling, or it may have been merely the reflex glow of a joy that made all other things seem insignificant.

As soon as might be after the meal Virginia slipped away, carrying the rifle, the cartridges, the matches, and the salt. She was cruelly frightened.

The night was providentially dark. No aurora threw its splendor across the dome, and only a few rare stars peeped between the light cirrus clouds. Virginia left behind her the buildings of the Post, she passed in safety the tin-steepled chapel and the church house; there remained only the Indian camp between her and the woods trail. At once the dogs began to bark and howl, the fierce *giddés* lifting their pointed noses to the sky. The girl hurried on, swinging far to the right through the grass. To her relief the camp did not respond to the summons. An old crone or so appeared in the flap of a teepee, eyes dazzled, to throw uselessly a billet of wood or a volley of Cree abuse at the animals nearest. In a moment Virginia entered the trail.

Here was no light at all. She had to proceed warily, feeling with her moccasins for the beaten pathway, to which she returned with infinite caution whenever she trod on grass or leaves. Though her sight was dulled, her hearing was not. A thousand scurrying noises swirled about her; a multitude of squeaks, whistles, snorts, and whines attested that she disturbed the forest creatures at their varied businesses; and underneath spoke an apparent dozen of terrifying voices which were in reality only the winds and the trees. Virginia knew that these things were not dangerous—that daylight would show them to be only deer-mice, hares, weasels, bats, and owls—nevertheless, they had their effect. For about her was cloying velvet blackness—not the closed-in blackness of a room, where one feels the embrace of the four walls, but the blackness of infinite space through which sweep mysterious currents of air. After a long time she turned sharp to the left. After a long time more she perceived a faint, opalescent glimmer in the distance ahead. This she knew to be the river.

She felt her way onward, still cautiously; then she choked back a scream and dropped her burden with a clatter to the ground. A dark figure seemed to have risen mysteriously at her side.

"I didn't mean to frighten you," said Ned Trent, in guarded tones. "I heard you coming. I thought you could hear me."

He picked up the fallen articles, running his hands over them rapidly.

"Good," he whispered. "I got some moccasins today—traded a few things I had in my pockets for them. I'm fixed."

"Have you a canoe?" she asked.

"Yes—here on the beach."

He preceded her down the few remaining yards of the trail. She followed, already desolated at the thought of parting, for the wilderness was very big. The bulk of the man partly blotted out the lucent spot where the river was—now his arm, now his head, now the breadth of his shoulders. This silhouette of him was dear to her, the sound of his movements, the faint stir of his breathing borne to her on the light breeze. Virginia's tender heart almost overflowed with longing and fear for him.

They emerged on a little slope and at once pushed the canoe into the current.

She accepted the aid of his hand for a moment, and sank to her place, facing him. He spurned lightly the shore, and so they were adrift.

In a moment they seemed to be floating on a vast vapor of night, infinitely remote from anywhere, surrounded by the silence that might have been before the world's beginning. A faint splash could have been a muskrat near at hand or a caribou far away. The paddle rose and dipped with a faint *swish, swish,* and the steersman's twist of it was taken up by the man's strong wrist so it did not click against the gunwale; the bow of the craft divided the waters with a murmuring so faint as to seem but the echo of a silence. Neither spoke. Virginia watched him, her heart too full for words; watched the full swing of his strong shoulders, the balance of his body at the hips, the poise of his head against the dull sky. In a moment more the parting would have to come. She dreaded it, and yet she looked forward to it with a hungry joy. Then he would say what she had seen in his eyes; then he would speak; then she would hear the words that should comfort her in the days of waiting. For a woman lives much for the present, and the moment's word is an important thing.

The man swung his paddle steadily, throwing into the strokes a wanton exuberance that showed how high his spirits ran. After a time, when they were well out from the shore, he took a deep breath of delight.

"Ah, you don't know how happy I am," he exulted, "you don't know! To be free, to play the game, to match my wits against theirs—ah, that is life!"

"I am sorry to see you go," she murmured, "very sorry. The days will be full of terror until I know you are safe."

"Oh, yes," he answered; "but I'll get there, and I shall tell it all to you at Quebec—at Quebec in August. It will be a brave tale! You will be there—surely?"

"Yes," said the girl, softly; "I will be there—surely."

"Good! Feel the wind on your cheek? It is from the Southland, where I am going. I have ventured—and I have not lost! It is something not to lose, when one has ventured against many. They have my goods—but I—"

"You?" repeated Virginia, as he hesitated.

"Ah, I don't go back empty-handed!" he cried. Her heart stood still, then leaped in anticipation of what he would say. Her soul hungered for the words, the words that should not only comfort her, but should be to her the excuse for many things. She saw him—shadowy, graceful against the dim gray of the river and sky—lean ever so slightly toward her. But then he straightened again to his paddle, and contented himself with repeating merely: "Quebec—in August, then."

The canoe grated. Ned Trent with an exclamation drove his paddle into the clay.

"Lucky the bottom is soft here," said he; "I did not realize we were so close ashore."

He drew the canoe up on the shelving beach, helped Virginia out, took his rifle, and so stood ready to depart.

"Leave the canoe just where we got in," he advised; "it is around the point, you see, and that may fool them a little."

"You are going," she said, dully. Then she came close to him and looked up at him with her wonderful eyes. "Good-by."

"Good-by," said he.

Was this to be all? Had he nothing more to tell her? Was the word to lack, the word she needed so much? She had given herself unreservedly into this man's hands, and at parting he had no more to say to her than "Good-by." Virginia's eyes were tearful, but she would not let him know that. She felt that her heart would break.

"Well, good-by," he said again after a moment, which he had spent inspecting the heavens. "Ah, you don't *know* what it is to be free! By tomorrow morning I shall be half-way to the Mattágami. I can hardly wait to see it, for then I am safe! And then next day—why, next day they won't know which of a dozen ways I've gone!" He was full of the future, man-fashion.

He took her hands, leaned over, and lightly kissed her on the mouth. Instantly Virginia became wildly and unreasonably angry. She could not have told herself why, but it was the lack of the word she had wanted so much, the pain of feeling that he could go like that, the thwarted bitterness of a longing that had grown stronger than she had even yet realized.

Instinctively she leaped into the canoe, sending it spinning from the bank.

"Ah, you had no *right* to do that!" she cried. "I gave you no *right*!"

Then, heedless of what he was saying, she began to paddle straight from the shore, weeping bitterly, her face upraised, her hair in her eyes, and the tears coursing unheeded down her cheeks.

CHAPTER FOURTEEN

Slower and slower her paddle dipped, lower and lower hung her head, faster and faster flowed her tears. The instinctive recoil, the passionate resentment had gone. In the bitterness of her spirit she knew not what she thought except that she would give her soul to see him again, to feel the touch of his lips once more. For she could not make herself believe that this would ever come to pass. He had gone like a phantom, like a dream, and the mists of life had closed about him, showing no sign. He had vanished, and at once she seemed to know that the episode was finished.

The canoe whispered against the soft clay bottom. She had arrived, though how the crossing had been made she could not have told. Slowly and sorrowfully she disembarked. Languidly she drew the light craft beyond the stream's eager fingers. Then, her forces at an end, she huddled down on the ground and gave herself up to sorrow.

The life of the forest went on as though she were not there. A big owl far off said hurriedly his *whoo-whoo-whoo*, as though he had the message to deliver and wanted to finish the task. A smaller owl near at hand cried *ko-ko-ko-oh* with the intonation of a tin horn. Across the river a lynx screamed, and was answered at once by the ululations of wolves. On the island the *giddés* howled defiance. Then from above, clear, spiritual, floated the whistle of shore birds arriving from the south. Close by sounded a rustle of leaves, a sharp squeak; a tragedy had been consummated, and the fierce little mink stared malevolently across the body of his victim at the motionless figure on the beach.

Virginia, drowned in grief, knew of none of these things. She was seeing again the clear brown face of the stranger, his curly brown hair, his steel eyes, and the swing of his graceful figure. Now he fronted the wondering *voyageurs*, one foot raised against the bow of the *brigade* canoe; now he stood straight and tall against the light of the sitting-room door; now he emptied the vials of his wrath and contempt on Archibald Crane's reverend head; now he passed in the darkness, singing gayly the *chanson de canôt*. But more fondly she saw him as he swept his hat to the ground on discovering her by the guns, as he bent his impassioned eyes on her in the dim lamplight of their first interview, as he tossed his hat aloft in the air when he had understood that she would be in Quebec. She hugged the visions to her, and wept over them softly, for she was now sure she would never see him again.

And she heard his voice, now laughing, now scornful, now mocking, now indignant, now rich and solemn with feeling. He flouted the people, he turned the shafts of his irony on her father, he scathed the minister, he laughed at Louis Placide awakened from his sleep, he sang, he told her of the land of desolation, he pleaded. She could hear him calling her name—although he had never spoken it—in low, tender tones, "Virginia! Virginia!" over and over again softly, as though his soul were crying through his lips.

Then somehow, in a manner not to be comprehended, it was borne in on her consciousness that he was indeed near her, and that he was indeed calling her name. And at once she made him out, standing dripping on the beach. A moment later she was in his arms.

"Ah!" he cried, in gladness; "you are here!"

He crushed her hungrily to him, unmindful of his wet clothes, kissing her eyes, her cheeks, her lips, her chin, even the fragrant corner of her throat exposed by the collar of her gown. She did not struggle.

"Oh!" she murmured, "my dear, my dear! Why did you come back? Why did you come?"

"Why did I come?" he repeated, passionately. "Why did I come? Can you ask that? How could I help but come? You must have known I would come. Surely you must have known! Didn't you hear me calling you when you paddled away? I came to get the right. I came to get your promise, your kisses, to hear you say the word, to get you! I thought you understood. It was all so clear to me. I thought you knew. That was why I was so glad to go, so eager to get away that I could not even realize I was parting from you—so I could the sooner reach Quebec—reach you! Don't you see how I felt? All this present was merely something to get over, to pass by, to put behind us until I got to Quebec in August—and you I looked forward so eagerly to that, I was so anxious to get away, I was desirous of hastening on to the time when things could be *sure*! Don't you understand?"

"Yes, I think I do," replied the girl, softly.

"And I thought of course you knew. I should not have kissed you otherwise."

"How could I know?" she sighed. "You said nothing, and, oh! I *wanted* so to hear!"

And singularly enough he said nothing now, but they stood facing each other hand in hand, while the great vibrant life they were now touching so closely filled their hearts and eyes, and left them faint. So they stood for hours or for seconds, they could not tell, spirit-hushed, ecstatic. The girl realized that they must part.

"You must go," she whispered brokenly, at last. "I do not want you to, but you must."

She smiled up at him with trembling lips that whispered to her soul that she must be brave.

"Now go," she nerved herself to say, releasing her hands.

"Tell me," he commanded.

"What?" she asked.

"What I most want to hear."

"I can tell you many things," said she, soberly, "but I do not know which of them you want to hear. Ah, Ned, I can tell you that you have come into a girl's life to make her very happy and very much afraid. And that is a solemn thing; is it not?"

"Yes," said he.

"And I can tell you that this can never be undone. That is a solemn thing, too, is it not?"

"Yes," said he.

"And that, according as you treat her, this girl will believe or not believe in the goodness of all men or the badness of all men. Ah, Ned, a woman's heart is fragile, and mine is in your keeping."

Her face was raised bravely and steadily to his. In the starlight it shone white and pathetic. And her eyes were two liquid wells of darkness in the shadow, and her half-parted lips were wistful and childlike.

The man caught both her hands, again looking down on her. Then he answered her, solemnly and humbly.

"Virginia," said he, "I am setting out on a perilous journey. As I deal with you, may God deal with me."

"Ah, that is as I like you," she breathed.

"Good-by," said he.

She raised her lips of her own accord, and he kissed them reverently.

"Good-by," she murmured.

He turned away with an effort and ran down the beach to the canoe.

"Good-by, good-by," she murmured, under her breath. "Ah, good-by! I love you! Oh, I do love you!"

Then suddenly from the bushes leaped dark figures. The still night was broken by the sound of a violent scuffle—blows—a fall. She heard Ned Trent's voice calling to her from the *mêlée*.

"Go back at once!" he commanded, clearly and steadily. "You can do no good. I order you to go home before they search the woods."

But she crouched in dazed terror, her pupils wide to the dim light. She saw them bind him, and stand waiting; she saw a canoe glide out of the darkness; she saw the occupants of the canoe disembark; she saw them exhibit her little rifle, and heard them explain in Cree, that they had followed the man swimming. Then she knew that the cause was lost, and fled as swiftly as she could through the forest.

CHAPTER FIFTEEN

Galen Albret had chosen to interrogate his recaptured prisoner alone. He sat again in the arm-chair of the Council Room.
The place was flooded with sun. It touched the high-lights of the
time-darkened, rough furniture, it picked out the brasses, it glori-
fied the whitewashed walls. In its uncompromising illumination
Me-en-gan, the bowsman, standing straight and tall and silent by
the door, studied his master's face and knew him to be deeply
angered.

For Galen Albret was at this moment called upon to deal with
a problem more subtle than any with which his policy had been
puzzled in thirty years. It was bad enough that, in repeated defiance of his authority, this stranger should persist in his attempt to
break the Company's monopoly; it was bad enough that he had,
when captured, borne himself with so impudent an air of assur-
ance; it was bad enough that he should have made open love to the
Factor's daughter, should have laughed scornfully in the Factor's
very face. But now the case had become grave. In some mysterious
manner he had succeeded in corrupting one of the Company's
servants. Treachery was therefore to be dealt with.

Some facts Galen Albret had well in hand. Others eluded him
persistently. He had, of course, known promptly enough of the
disappearance of a canoe, and had thereupon dispatched his
Indians to the recapture. The Reverend Archibald Crane had
reported that two figures had been seen in the act of leaving camp,
one by the river, the other by the Woods Trail. But here the Factor's investigations encountered a check. The rifle brought in by
his Indians, to his bewilderment, he recognized not at all. His
repeated cross-questionings, when they touched on the question
of Ned Trent's companion, got no farther than the Cree wooden
stolidity. No, they had seen no one, neither presence, sign, nor
trail. But Galen Albret, versed in the psychology of his savage
allies, knew they lied. He suspected them of clan loyalty to one of
their own number; and yet they had never failed him before. Now,
his heavy revolver at his right hand, he interviewed Ned Trent,
alone, except for the Indian by the portal.

As with the Indians, his cross-examination had borne scant

results. The best of his questions but involved him in a maze of baffling surmises. Gradually his anger had mounted, until now the Indian at the door knew by the wax-like appearance of the more prominent places on his deeply carved countenance that he had nearly reached the point of outbreak.

Swiftly, like the play of rapiers, the questions and answers broke across the still room.

"You had aid," the Factor asserted, positively.

"You think so?"

"My Indians say you were alone. But where did you get this rifle?"

"I stole it."

"You were alone?"

Ned Trent paused for a barely appreciable instant. It was not possible that the Indians had failed to establish the girl's presence, and he feared a trap. Then he caught the expressive eye of Me-en-gan at the door. Evidently Virginia had friends.

"I was alone," he repeated, confidently.

"That is a lie. For though my Indians were deceived, two people were observed by my clergyman to leave the Post immediately before I sent out to your capture. One rounded the island in a canoe; the other took the Woods Trail."

"Bully for the Church," replied Trent, imperturbably. "Better promote him to your scouts."

"Who was that second person?"

"Do you think I will tell you?"

"I think I'll find means to make you tell me!" burst out the Factor.

Ned Trent was silent.

"If you'll tell me the name of that man I'll let you go free. I'll give you a permit to trade in the country. It touches my authority—my discipline. The affair becomes a precedent. It is vital."

Ned Trent fixed his eyes on the bay and hummed a little air, half turning his shoulder to the older man.

The latter's face blazed with suppressed fury. Twice his hand rested almost convulsively on the butt of his heavy revolver.

"Ned Trent," he cried, harshly, at last, "pay attention to me.

I've had enough of this. I swear if you do not tell me what I want to know within five minutes, I'll hang you today!"

The young man spun on his heel.

"Hanging!" he cried. "You cannot mean that?"

The Free Trader measured him up and down, saw that his purpose was sincere, and turned slowly pale under the bronze of his out-of-door tan. Hanging is always a dreadful death, but in the Far North it carries an extra stigma of ignominy with it, inasmuch as it is resorted to only with the basest malefactors. Shooting is the usual form of execution for all but the most despicable crimes. He turned away with a little gesture.

"Well!" cried Albret.

Ned Trent locked his lips in a purposeful straight line of silence. To such an outrage there could be nothing to say. The Factor jerked his watch to the table.

"I said five minutes," he repeated. "I mean it."

The young man leaned against the side of the window, his arms folded, his back to the room. Outside, the varied life of the Post went forward under his eyes. He even noted with a surface interest the fact that out across the river a loon was floating, and remarked that never before had he seen one of those birds so far north. Galen Albret struck the table with the flat of his hand.

"Done!" he cried, "This is the last chance I shall give you. Speak at this instant or accept the consequences!"

Ned Trent turned sharply, as though breaking a thread that bound him to the distant prospect beyond the window. For an instant he stared enigmatically at his opponent. Then in the sweetest tones,

"Oh, go to the devil!" said he, and began to walk deliberately toward the older man.

There lay between the window and the head of the table perhaps a dozen ordinary steps, for the room was large. The young man took them slowly, his eyes fixed with burning intensity on the seated figure, the muscles of his locomotion contracting and relaxing with the smooth, stealthy continuity of a cat. Galen Albret again laid hand on his revolver.

"Come no nearer," he commanded.

Me-en-gan left the door and glided along the wall. But the

table intervened between him and the Free Trader.

The latter paid no attention to the Factor's command. Galen Albret suddenly raised his weapon from the table.

"Stop, or I'll fire!" he cried, sharply.

"I mean just that," said Ned Trent between his clenched teeth.

But ten feet separated the two men. Galen Albret levelled the revolver. Ned Trent, watchful, prepared to spring. Me-en-gan, near the foot of the table, gathered himself for attack.

Then suddenly the Free Trader relaxed his muscles, straightened his back, and returned deliberately to the window. Facing about in astonishment to discover the reason for this sudden change of decision, the other two men looked into the face of Virginia Albret, standing in the doorway of the other room.

"Father!" she cried.

"You must go back," said Ned Trent, speaking clearly and collectedly, in the hope of imposing his will on her obvious excitement. "This is not an affair in which you should interfere. Galen Albret, send her away."

The Factor had turned squarely in his heavy arm-chair to regard the girl, a frown on his brows.

"Virginia," he commanded, in deliberate, stern tones of authority, "leave the room. You have nothing to do with this case, and I do not desire your interference."

Virginia stepped bravely beyond the portals, and stopped. Her fingers were nervously interlocked, her lip trembled, in her cheeks the color came and went, but her eyes met her father's, unfaltering.

"I have more to do with it than you think," she replied.

Instantly Ned Trent was at the table. "I really think this has gone far enough," he interposed. "We have had our interview, and come to a decision. Miss Albret must not be permitted to exaggerate a slight sentiment of pity into an interest in my affairs. If she knew that such a demonstration only made it worse for me I am sure she would say no more." He looked at her appealingly across the Factor's shoulder.

Me-en-gan was already holding open the door. "You come," he smiled, beseechingly.

But the Factor's suspicions were aroused.

"There is something in this," he decided. "I think you may stay, Virginia."

"You are right," broke in the young man, desperately. "There is something in it. Miss Albret knows who gave me the rifle, and she was about to inform you of his identity. There is no need in subjecting her to that distasteful ordeal. I am now ready to confess to you. I beg you will ask her to leave the room."

Galen Albret, in the midst of these warring intentions, had sunk into his customary impassive calm. The light had died from his eyes, the expression from his face, the energy from his body. He sat, an inert mass, void of initiative, his intelligence open to what might be brought to his notice.

"Virginia, this is true?" his heavy, dead voice rumbled through his beard. "You know who aided this man?"

Ned Trent mutely appealed to her; her glance answered his.

"Yes, father," she replied.

"Who?"

"I did."

A dead silence fell on the room. Galen Albret's expression and attitude did not change. Through dull, lifeless eyes, from behind the heavy mask of his waxen face and white beard, he looked steadily out upon nothing. Along either arm of the chair stretched his own arms limp and heavy with inertia. In suspense the other three inmates of the place watched him, waiting for some change. It did not come. Finally his lips moved.

"You?" he muttered, questioningly.

"I," she repeated.

Another silence fell.

"Why?" he asked at last.

"Because it was an unjust thing. Because we could not think of taking a life in that way, without some reason for it."

"Why?" he persisted, taking no account of her reply.

Virginia let her gaze slowly rest on the Free Trader, and her eyes filled with a world of tenderness and trust.

"Because I love him," said she, softly.

CHAPTER SIXTEEN

After an instant Galen Albret turned slowly his massive head and looked at her. He made no other movement, yet she staggered back as though she had received a violent blow on the chest.

"Father!" she gasped.

Still slowly, gropingly, he arose to his feet, holding tight to the edge of the table. Behind him unheeded the rough-built armchair crashed to the floor. He stood there upright and motionless, looking straight before him, his face formidable. At first his speech was disjointed. The words came in widely punctuated gasps. Then, as the wave of his emotion rolled back from the poise into which the first shock of anger had thrown it, it escaped through his lips in a constantly increasing stream of bitter words.

"You—you love him," he cried. "You—my daughter! You have been—a traitor—to me! You have dared—dared—deny that which my whole life has affirmed! My own flesh and blood—when I thought the nearest *mètis* of them all more loya.! You love this man—this man who has insulted me, mocked me! You have taken his part against me! You have deliberately placed yourself in the class of those I would hang for such an offence! If you were not my daughter I would hang you. Hang my own child!" Suddenly his rage flared. "You little fool! Do you dare set your judgment against mine? Do you dare interfere where I think well? Do you dare deny my will? By the eternal, I'll show you, old as you are, that you have still a father! Get to your room! Out of my sight!" He took two steps forward, and so his eye fell on Ned Trent. He uttered a scream of rage, and reached for the pistol. Fortunately the abruptness of his movement when he arose had knocked it to the floor, so now in the blindness of a red anger he could not see it. He shrieked out an epithet and jumped forward, his arm drawn to strike. Ned Trent leaped back into an attitude of defence.

All three of those present had many times seen Galen Albret possessed by his noted fits of anger, so striking in contrast to his ordinary contained passivity. But always, though evidently in a white heat of rage and given to violent action and decision, he had retained the clearest command of his faculties, issuing coherent and dreaded orders to those about him. Now he had become a raging wild beast. And for the spectators the sight had all the horror of the unprecedented.

But the younger man, too, had gradually heated to the point where his ordinary careless indifference could give off sparks. The interview had been baffling, the threats real and unjust, the turn of affairs when Virginia Albret entered the room most exasperating on the side of the undesirable and unforeseen. In foiled escape, in thwarted expedient, his emotions had been many times excited, and then eddied back on themselves. The potentialities of as blind an anger as that of Galen Albret were in him. It only needed a touch to loose the flood. The physical threat of a blow supplied that touch. As the two men faced each other both were ripe for the extreme of recklessness.

But while Galen Albret looked to nothing less than murder, the Free-Trader's individual genius turned to dead defiance and resistance of will. While Galen Albret's countenance reflected the height of passion, Trent was as smiling and cool and debonair as though he had at that moment received from the older man an extraordinary and particular favor. Only his eyes shot a baleful blue flame, and his words, calmly enough delivered, showed the extent to which his passion had cast policy to the winds.

"Don't go too far! I warn you!" said he.

As though the words had projected him bodily forward, Galen Albret sprang to deliver his blow. The Free Trader ducked rapidly, threw his shoulder across the middle of the older man's body, and by the very superiority of his position forced his antagonist to give ground. That the struggle would have then continued body to body there can be no doubt, had it not been for the fact that the Factor's retrogressive movement brought his knees sharply against the edge of a chair standing near the side of the table. Albret lost his balance, wavered, and finally sat down violently. Ned Trent promptly pinned him by the shoulder into powerless immobility. Me-en-gan had possessed himself of the fallen pistol, but beyond keeping a generally wary eye out for dangerous developments, did not offer to interfere. Your Indian is in such a crisis a disciplinarian, and he had received no orders.

"Now," said Ned Trent, acidly, "I think this will stop right here. You do not cut a very good figure, my dear sir," he laughed a little. "You haven't cut a very good figure from the beginning, you know. You forbade me to do various things, and I have done them all. I traded with your Indians. I came and went in your country. Do you think I have not been here often before I was caught? And you forbade me to see your daughter again. I saw her that very evening, and the next morning and the next evening."

He stood, still holding Galen Albret immovably in the chair, looking steadily and angrily into the Factor's eyes, driving each word home with the weight of his contained passion. The girl touched his arm.

"Hush! oh, hush!" she cried in a panic. "Do not anger him further!"

"When you forbade me to make love to her," he continued, unheeding, "I laughed at you." With a sudden, swift motion of his left arm he drew her to him and touched her forehead with his lips. "Look! Your commands have been rather ridiculous, sir. I seem to have had the upper hand of you from first to last. Incidentally you have my life. Oh, welcome! That is small pay and little satisfaction."

He threw himself from the Factor and stepped back.

Galen Albret sat still without attempting to renew the struggle. The enforced few moments of inaction had restored to him his self-control. He was still deeply angered, but the insanity of rage had left him. Outwardly he was himself again. Only a rapid heaving of his chest answered Ned Trent's quick breathing, as the two men glared defiantly at each other in the pause that followed.

"Very well, sir," said the Factor, curtly, at last. "Your time is over. I find it unnecessary to hang you. You will start on your *Longue Traverse* today."

"Oh!" cried Virginia, in a low voice of agony, and fluttered to her lover's side.

"Hush! hush!" he soothed her. "There is a chance."

"You think so?" broke in Galen Albret, harshly. And looking at his set face and blazing eyes, they saw that there was no chance. The Free Trader shrugged his shoulders.

"You are going to do this thing, father," appealed Virginia, "after what I have told you?"

"My mind is made up."

"I shall not survive him, father!" she threatened, in a low voice. Then, as the Factor did not respond, "Do not misunderstand me. I do not intend to survive him."

"Silence! silence! silence!" cried Galen Albret, in a crescendo outburst. "Silence! I will not be gainsaid! You have made your choice! You are no longer a daughter of mine!"

"Father!" cried Virginia, faintly, her lips going pale.

"Don't speak to me! Don't look at me! Get out of here! Get out of the place! I won't have you here another day—another hour! By—"

The girl hesitated for a moment, then ran to him, sinking on her knees, and clasping his hand.

"Father," she pleaded, "you are not yourself. This has been very trying to you. Tomorrow you will be sorry. But then it will be too late. Think, while there is yet time. He has not committed a crime. You yourself told me he was a man of intelligence and daring—a gentleman; and surely, though he has been hasty, he has acted with a brave spirit through it all. See, he will promise you to go away quietly, to say nothing of all this, never to come into this country again without your permission. He will do this if I ask him, for he loves me. Look at me, father. Are you going to treat your little girl so—your Virginia? You have never refused me anything before. And this is the greatest thing in all my life." She held his hand to her cheek and stroked it, murmuring little feminine, caressing phrases, secure in her power of witchery, which had never failed her before. The sound of her own voice reassured her, the quietude of the man she pleaded with. A lifetime of petting, of indulgence, threw its soothing influence over her perturbation, convincing her that somehow all this storm and stress must be phantasmagoric—a dream from which she was even now awakening into a clearer day of happiness. "For you love me, father," she concluded, and looked up daintily, with a pathetic, coquettish tilt of her fair head, to peer into his face.

Galen Albret snarled like a wild beast, throwing aside the girl, as he did the chair in which he had been sitting. Ned Trent caught her, reeling, in his arms.

For, as is often the case with passionate but strong temperaments, though the Factor had attained a certain calm of control, the turmoil of his deeper anger had not been in the least stilled. Over it a crust of determination had formed—the determination to make an end by the directest means in his autocratic power of this galling opposition. The girl's pleading, instead of appealing to him, had in reality but stirred his fury the more profoundly. It had added a new fuel element to the fire. Heretofore his consciousness had felt merely the thwarting of his pride, his authority, his right to loyalty. Now his daughter's entreaty brought home to him the bitter realization that he had been attained on another side—that of his family affection. This man had also killed for him his only child. For the child had renounced him, had thrust him outside herself into the lonely and ruined temple of his pride. At the first thought his face twisted with emotion, then hardened to cold malice.

"Love you!" he cried. "Love you! An unnatural child! An ingrate! One who turns from me so lightly!" He laughed bitterly, eyeing her with chilling scrutiny. "You dare recall my love for you!" Suddenly he stood upright, levelling a heavy, trembling arm at her. "You think an appeal to my love will save him! Fool!"

Virginia's breath caught in her throat. She straightened, clutched the neckband of her gown. Then her head fell slowly forward. She had fainted in her lover's arms.

They stood exactly so for an appreciable interval, bewildered by the suddenness of this outcome; Galen Albret's hand outstretched in denunciation; the girl like a broken lily, supported in the young man's arms; he searching her face passionately for a sign of life; Me-en-gan, straight and sorrowful, again at the door.

Then the old man's arm dropped slowly. His gaze wavered. The lines of his face relaxed. Twice he made an effort to turn away. All at once his stubborn spirit broke; he uttered a cry, and sprang forward to snatch the unconscious form hungrily into his bear clasp, searching the girl's face, muttering incoherent things.

"Quick!" he cried, aloud, the guttural sounds jostling one another in his throat. "Get Wishkobun, quick!"

Ned Trent looked at him with steady scorn, his arms folded.

"Ah!" he dropped distinctly in deliberate monosyllables across the surcharged atmosphere of the scene. "So it seems you have found your heart, my friend!"

Galen Albret glared wildly at him over the girl's fair head.

"She is my daughter," he mumbled.

CHAPTER SEVENTEEN

They carried the unconscious girl into the dim-lighted apartment of the curtained windows, and laid her on the divan. Wishkobun, hastily summoned, unfastened the girl's dress at the throat.

"It is a faint," she announced in her own tongue. "She will recover in a few minutes; I will get some water."

Ned Trent wiped the moisture from his forehead with his handkerchief. The danger he had undergone coolly, but this overcame his iron self-control. Galen Albret, like an anxious bear, weaved back and forth the length of the couch. In him the rumble of the storm was but just echoing into distance.

"Go into the next room," he growled at the Free Trader, when finally he noticed the latter's presence.

Ned Trent hesitated.

"Go, I say!" snarled the Factor. "You can do nothing here." He followed the young man to the door, which he closed with his own hand, and then turned back to the couch on which his daughter lay. In the middle of the floor his foot clicked on some small object. Mechanically he picked it up.

It proved to be a little silver match-safe of the sort universally used in the Far North. Evidently the Free Trader had flipped it from his pocket with his handkerchief. The Factor was about to thrust it into his own pocket, when his eye caught lettering roughly carved across one side. Still mechanically, he examined it more closely. The lettering was that of a man's name. The man's name was Graehme Stewart.

Without thinking of what he did, he dropped the object on the small table, and returned anxiously to the girl's side, cursing the tardiness of the Indian woman. But in a moment Wishkobun returned.

"Will she recover?" asked the Factor, distracted at the woman's deliberate examination.

The latter smiled her indulgent, slow smile. "But surely," she assured him in her own tongue, "it is no more than if she cut her finger. In a few breaths she will recover. Now I will go to the house of the Cockburn for a morsel of the sweet wood[1] which she must smell." She looked her inquiry for permission.

"Sagaamig—go," assented Albret.

Relieved in mind, he dropped into a chair. His eye caught the little silver match-safe. He picked it up and fell to staring at the rudely carved letters.

He found that he was alone with his daughter—and the thoughts aroused by the dozen letters of a man's name.

All his life long he had been a hard man. His commands had been autocratic; his anger formidable; his punishments severe, and sometimes cruel. The quality of mercy was with him tenuous and weak. He knew this, and if he did not exactly glory in it, he was at least indifferent to its effect on his reputation with others. But always he had been just. The victims of his displeasure might complain that his retributive measures were harsh, that his forgiveness could not be evoked by even the most extenuating of circumstances, but not that his anger had ever been baseless or the punishment undeserved. Thus he had held always his own self-respect, and from his self-respect had proceeded his iron and effective rule.

So in the case of the young man with whom now his thoughts were occupied. Twice he had warned him from the country without the punishment which the third attempt rendered imperative. The events succeeding his arrival at Conjuror's House warmed the Factor's anger to the heat of almost preposterous retribution perhaps—for after all a man's life is worth something, even in the wilds—but it was actually retribution, and not merely a ruthless proof of power. It might be justice as only the Factor saw it, but it was still essentially justice—in the broader sense that to each act had followed a definite consequence. Although another might have condemned his conduct as unnecessarily harsh, Galen Albret's conscience was satisfied and at rest.

Nor had his resolution been permanently affected by either

1   Camphor.

the girl's threat to make away with herself or by his momentary softening when she had fainted. The affair was thereby complicated, but that was all. In the sincerity of the threat he recognized his own iron nature, and was perhaps a little pleased at its manifestation. He knew she intended to fulfil her promise not to survive her lover, but at the moment this did not reach his fears; it only aroused further his dogged opposition.

The Free Trader's speech as he left the room, however, had touched the one flaw in Galen Albret's confidence of righteousness. Wearied with the struggles and the passions he had undergone, his brain numbed, his will for the moment in abeyance, he seated himself and contemplated the images those two words had called up.

Graehme Stewart! That man he had first met at Fort Rae over twenty years ago. It was but just after he had married Virginia's mother. At once his imagination, with the keen pictorial power of those who have dwelt long in the Silent Places, brought forward the other scene—that of his wooing. He had driven his dogs into Fort la Cloche after a hard day's run in seventy-five degrees of frost. Weary, hungry, half-frozen, he had staggered into the fire-lit room. Against the blaze he had caught for a moment a young girl's profile, lost as she turned her face toward him in startled question of his entrance. Men had cared for his dogs. The girl had brought him hot tea. In the corner of the fire they two had whispered one to the other—the already grizzled traveller of the silent land, the fresh, brave north-maiden. At midnight, their parkas drawn close about their faces in the fearful cold, they had met outside the inclosure of the Post. An hour later they were away under the aurora for Qu'Apelle. Galen Albret's nostrils expanded as he heard the *crack, crack, crack* of the remorseless dog-whip whose sting drew him away from the vain pursuit. After the marriage at Qu'Apelle they had gone a weary journey to Rae, and there he had first seen Graehme Stewart.

Fort Rae is on the northwestward arm of the Great Slave Lake in the country of the Dog Ribs, only four degrees under the Arctic Circle. It is a dreary spot, for the Barren Grounds are near. Men see only the great lake, the great sky, the great gray country. They become moody, fanciful. In the face of the silence they have little to say. At Fort Rae were old Jock Wilson, the Chief Trader; Father Bonat, the priest; Andrew Levoy, the *mètis* clerk; four Dog Rib teepees; Galen Albret and his bride; and Graehme Stewart.

Jock Wilson was sixty-five; Father Bonat had no age; Andrew Levoy possessed the years of dour silence. Only Graehme Stewart and Elodie, bride of Albret, were young. In the great gray country their lives were like spots of color on a mist. Galen Albret finally became jealous.

At first there was nothing to be done; but finally Levoy brought to the older man proof of the younger's guilt. The harsh traveller bowed his head and wept. But since he loved Elodie more than himself which was perhaps the only redeeming feature of this sorry business—he said nothing, nor did more than to journey south to Edmonton, leaving the younger man alone in Fort Rae to the White Silence. But his soul was stirred.

In the course of nature and of time Galen Albret had a daughter, but lost a wife. It was no longer necessary for him to leave his wrong unavenged. Then began a series of baffling hindrances which resulted finally in his stooping to means repugnant to his open sense of what was due himself. At the first he could not travel to his enemy because of the child in his care; when finally he had succeeded in placing the little girl where he would be satisfied to leave her, he himself was suddenly and peremptorily called east to take a post in Rupert's Land. He could not disobey and remain in the Company, and the Company was more to him than life or revenge. The little girl he left in Sacré Coeur of Quebec; he himself took up his residence in the Hudson Bay country. After a few years, becoming lonely for his own flesh and blood, he sent for his daughter. There, as Factor, he gained a vast power; and this power he turned into the channels of his hatred. Graehme Stewart felt always against him the hand of influence. His posts in the Company's service became intolerable. At length, in indignation against continued injustice, oppression, and insult, he resigned, broken in fortune and in prospects. He became one of the earliest Free Traders on the Saskatchewan, devoting his energies to enraged opposition of the Company which had wronged him. In the space of three short years he had met a violent and striking death; for the early days of the Free Trader were adventurous.

Galen Albret's revenge had struck home.

Then in after years the Factor had again met with Andrew Levoy. The man staggered into Conjuror's House late at night. He had started from Winnipeg to descend the Albany River, but had met with mishap and starvation. One by one his dogs had died. In some blind fashion he pushed on for days after his strength and sanity had left him. Mu-hi-kun had brought him in. His toes and fingers had frozen and dropped off; his face was a mask of black frost-bitten flesh, in which deep fissures opened to the raw. He had gone snow-blind. Scarcely was he recognizable as a human being.

From such a man in extremity could come nothing but the truth, so Galen Albret believed him. Before Andrew Levoy died that night he told of his deceit. The Factor left the room with the weight of a crime on his conscience. For Graehme Stewart had been innocent of any wrong toward him or his bride.

Such was the story Galen Albret saw in the little silver match-box. That was the one flaw in his consciousness of righteousness; the one instance in a long career when his ruthless acts of punishment or reprisal had not rested on rigid justice, and by the irony of fate the one instance had touched him very near. Now here before him was his enemy's son—he wondered that he had not discovered the resemblance before—and he was about to visit on him the severest punishment in his power. Was not this an opportunity vouchsafed him to repair his ancient fault, to cleanse his conscience of the one sin of the kind it would acknowledge?

But then over him swept the same blur of jealousy that had resulted in Graehme Stewart's undoing. This youth wooed his daughter; he had won her affections away. Strangely enough Galen Albret confused the new and the old; again youth cleaved to youth, leaving age apart. Age felt fiercely the desire to maintain its own. The Factor crushed the silver match-box between his great palms and looked up. His daughter lay before him, still, lifeless. Deliberately he rested his chin on his hands and contemplated her.

The room, as always, was full of contrast; shafts of light, dust-moted, bewildering, crossed from the embrasured windows, throwing high-lights into prominence and shadows into impenetrable darkness. They rendered the gray-clad figure of the girl vague and ethereal, like a mist above a stream; they darkened the dull-hued couch on which she rested into a liquid, impalpable black; they hazed the draped background of the corner into a far-reaching distance; so that finally to Galen Albret, staring with hypnotic intensity, it came to seem that he looked upon a pure and disembodied spirit sleeping sweetly—cradled on illimitable space. The ordinary and familiar surroundings all disappeared. His consciousness accepted nothing but the cameo profile of marble white, the nimbus of golden haze about the head, the mist-like suggestion of a body, and again the clear marble spot of the hands. All else was a background of modulated depths.

So gradually the old man's spirit, wearied by the stress of the last hour, turned in on itself and began to create. The cameo profile, the mist-like body, the marble hands remained; but now Galen Albret saw other things as well. A dim, rare perfume was wafted from some unseen space; indistinct flashes of light spotted the darknesses; faint swells of music lifted the silence intermittently. These things were small and still, and under the external consciousness—like the voices one may hear beneath the roar of a tumbling rapid—but gradually they defined themselves. The perfume came to Galen Albret's nostrils on the wings of incensed smoke; the flashes of light steadied to the ovals of candle flames; the faint swells of music blended into grand-breathed organ chords. He felt about him the dim awe of the church, he saw the tapers burning at head and foot, the clear, calm face of the dead, smiling faintly that at last it should be no more disturbed. So had he looked all one night and all one day in the long time ago. The Factor stretched his arms out to the figure on the couch, but he called upon his wife, gone these twenty years.

"Elodie! Elodie!" he murmured, softly.

She had never known it, thank God, but he had wronged her too. In all sorrow and sweet heavenly pity he had believed that her youth had turned to the youth of the other man. It had not been so. Did he not owe her, too, some reparation?

As though in answer to his appeal, or perhaps that merely the sound of a human voice had broken the last shreds of her swoon, the girl moved slightly. Galen Albret did not stir. Slowly Virginia turned her head, until finally her wandering eyes met his, fixed on her with passionate intensity. For a moment she stared at him, then comprehension came to her along with memory. She cried out, and sat upright in one violent motion.

"He! He!" she cried. "Is he gone?"

Instantly Galen Albret had her in his arms.

"It is all right," he soothed, drawing her close to his great breast. "All right. You are my own little girl."

CHAPTER EIGHTEEN

For perhaps ten minutes Ned Trent lingered near the door of the Council Room until he had assured himself that Virginia was in no serious danger. Then he began to pace the room, examining minutely the various objects that ornamented it. He paused longest at the full-length portrait of Sir George Simpson, the Company's great traveller, with his mild blue eyes, his kindly face, denying the potency of his official frown, his snowy hair and whiskers. The painted man and the real man looked at each other inquiringly. The latter shook his head.

"You travelled the wild country far," said he, thoughtfully. "You knew many men of many lands. And wherever you went they tell me you made friends. And yet, as you embodied this Company to all these people, and so made for the fanatical loyalty that is destroying me, I suppose you and I are enemies!" He shrugged his shoulders whimsically and turned away.

Thence he cast a fleeting glance out the window at the long reach of the Moose and the blue bay gleaming in the distance. He tried the outside door. It was locked. Taken with a new idea he proceeded at once to the third door of the apartment. It opened.

He found himself in a small and much-littered room containing a desk, two chairs, a vast quantity of papers, a stuffed bird or so, and a row of account-books. Evidently the Factor's private office.

Ned Trent returned to the main room and listened intently for several minutes. After that he ran back to the office and began hastily to open and rummage, one after another, the drawers of the desk. He discovered and concealed several bits of string, a desk-knife, and a box of matches. Then he uttered a guarded exclamation of delight. He had found a small revolver, and with it part of a box of cartridges.

"A chance!" he exulted: "a chance!"

The game would be desperate. He would be forced first of all to seek out and kill the men detailed to shadow him—a toy revolver against rifles; white man against trained savages. And after that he would have, with the cartridges remaining, to assure his subsistence. Still it was a chance.

He closed the drawers and the door, and resumed his seat in the arm-chair by the council table.

For over an hour thereafter he awaited the next move in the game. He was already swinging up the pendulum arc. The case did not appear utterly hopeless. He resolved, through Me-en-gan, whom he divined as a friend of the girl's, to smuggle a message to Virginia bidding her hope. Already his imagination had conducted him to Quebec, when in August he would search her out and make her his own.

Soon one of the Indian servants entered the room for the purpose of conducting him to a smaller apartment, where he was left alone for some time longer. Food was brought him. He ate heartily, for he considered that wise. Then at last the summons for which he had been so long in readiness. Me-en-gan himself entered the room, and motioned him to follow.

Ned Trent had already prepared his message on the back of an envelope, writing it with the lead of a cartridge. He now pressed the bit of paper into the Indian's palm.

"For O-mi-mi," he explained.

Me-en-gan bored him through with his bead-like eyes of the surface lights.

"Nin nissitotam," he agreed after a moment.

He led the way. Ned Trent followed through the narrow, uncarpeted hall with the faded photograph of Westminster, down the crooked steep stairs with the creaking degrees, and finally into the Council Room once more, with its heavy rafters, its two fireplaces, its long table, and its narrow windows.

"Beka—wait!" commanded Me-en-gan, and left him.

Ned Trent had supposed he was being conducted to the canoe which should bear him on the first stage of his long journey, but now he seemed condemned again to take up the wearing uncertainty of inaction. The interval was not long, however. Almost immediately the other door opened and the Factor entered.

His movements were abrupt and impatient, for with whatever grace such a man yields to his better instincts the actual carrying out of their conditions is a severe trial. For one thing it is a species of emotional nakedness, invariably repugnant to the self-contained. Ned Trent, observing this and misinterpreting its cause, hugged the little revolver to his side with grim satisfaction. The interview was likely to be stormy. If worst came to worst, he was at least assured of reprisal before his own end.

The Factor walked directly to the head of the table and his customary arm-chair, in which he disposed himself.

"Sit down," he commanded the younger man, indicating a chair at his elbow.

The latter warily obeyed.

Galen Albret hesitated appreciably. Then, as one would make a plunge into cold water, quickly, in one motion, he laid on the table something over which he held his hand.

"You are wondering why I am interviewing you again," said he. "It is because I have become aware of certain things. When you left me a few hours ago you dropped this." He moved his hand to one side. The silver match-safe lay on the table.

"Yes, it is mine," agreed Ned Trent.

"On one side is carved a name."

"Yes."

"Whose?"

The Free Trader hesitated. "My father's," he said, at last.

"I thought that must be so. You will understand when I tell you that at one time I knew him very well."

"You knew my father?" cried Ned Trent, excitedly.

"Yes. At Fort Rae, and elsewhere. But I do not remember you."

"I was brought up at Winnipeg," the other explained.

"Once," pursued Galen Albret, "I did your father a wrong, unintentionally, but nevertheless a great wrong. For that reason and others I am going to give you your life."

"What wrong?" demanded Ned Trent, with dawning excitement.

"I forced him from the Company."

"You!"

"Yes, I. Proof was brought me that he had won from me my young wife. It could not be doubted. I could not kill him. Afterward the man who received me confessed. He is now dead."

Ned Trent, gasping, rose slowly to his feet. One hand stole inside his jacket and clutched the butt of the little pistol.

"You did that," he cried, hoarsely. "You tell me of it yourself?

Do you wish to know the real reason for my coming into this country, why I have traded in defiance of the Company throughout the whole Far North? I have thought my father was persecuted by a body of men, and though I could not do much, still I have accomplished what I could to avenge him. Had I known that a single man had done this—and you are that man!"

He came a step nearer. Galen Albret regarded him steadily.

"If I had known this before, I should never have rested until I had hunted you down, until I had killed you, even in the midst of your own people!" cried the Free Trader at last.

Galen Albret drew his heavy revolver and laid it on the table.

"Do so now," he said, quietly.

A pause fell on them, pregnant with possibility. The Free Trader dropped his head.

"No," he groaned. "No, I cannot. She stands in the way!"

"So that, after all," concluded the Factor, in a gentler tone than he had yet employed, "we two shall part peaceably. I have wronged you greatly, though without intention. Perhaps one balances the other. We will let it pass."

"Yes," agreed Ned Trent with an effort, "we will let it pass."

They mused in silence, while the Factor drummed on the table with the stubby fingers of his right hand.

"I am dispatching today," he announced curtly at length, "the Abítibi *brigade*. Matters of importance brought by runner from Rupert's House force me to do so a month earlier than I had expected. I shall send you out with that *brigade*."

"Very well."

"You will find your packs and arms in the canoe, quite intact."

"Thank you."

The Factor examined the young man's face with some deliberation.

"You love my daughter truly?" he asked, quietly.

"Yes," replied Ned Trent, also quietly.

"That is well, for she loves you. And," went on the old man, throwing his massive head back proudly, "my people love well! I won her mother in a day, and nothing could stay us. God be thanked, you are a man and brave and clean. Enough of that! I place the *brigade* under your command! You must be responsible for it, for I am sending no other white—the crew are Indians and *mètis*."

"All right," agreed Ned Trent, indifferently.

"My daughter you will take to Sacré Coeur at Quebec."

"Virginia!" cried the young man.

"I am sending her to Quebec. I had not intended doing so until July, but the matters from Rupert's House make it imperative now."

"Virginia goes with me?"

"Yes."

"You consent? You—"

"Young man," said Galen Albret, not unkindly, "I give my daughter in your charge; that is all. You must take her to Sacré Coeur. And you must be patient. Next year I shall resign, for I am getting old, and then we shall see. That is all I can tell you now."

He arose abruptly.

"Come," said he, "they are waiting."

They threw wide the door and stepped out into the open. A breeze from the north brought a draught of air like cold water in its refreshment. The waters of the North sparkled and tossed in the silvery sun. Ned Trent threw his arms wide in the physical delight of a new freedom.

But his companion was already descending the steps. He followed across the square grass plot to the two bronze guns. A noise of peoples came down the breeze. In a moment he saw them—the varied multitude of the Post—gathered to speed the *brigade* on its distant journey.

The little beach was crowded with the Company's people and with Indians, talking eagerly, moving hither and yon in a shifting kaleidoscope of brilliant color. Beyond the shore floated the long canoe, with its curving ends and its emblazonment of the five-pointed stars. Already its baggage was aboard, its crew in place, ten men in whose caps slanted long, graceful feathers, which proved them boatmen of a factor. The women sat amidships.

When Galen Albret reached the edge of the plateau he stopped, and laid his hand on the young man's arm. As yet they were unperceived. Then a single man caught sight of them. He spoke to another; the two informed still others. In an instant the bright colors were dotted with upturned faces.

"Listen," said Galen Albret, in his resonant chest-tones of authority. "This is my son, and he must be obeyed. I give to him the command of this *brigade*. See to it."

Without troubling himself further as to the crowd below, Galen Albret turned to his companion.

"I will say good-by," said he, formally.

"Good-by," replied Ned Trent.

"All is at peace between us?"

The Free Trader looked long into the man's sad eyes. The hard, proud spirit, bowed in knightly expiation of its one fault, for the first time in a long life of command looked out in petition.

"All is at peace," repeated Ned Trent.

They clasped hands. And Virginia, perceiving them so, threw them a wonderful smile.

CHAPTER NINETEEN

Instantly the spell of inaction broke. The crowd recommenced its babel of jests, advices, and farewells. Ned Trent swung down the bank to the shore. The boatmen fixed the canoe on the very edge of floating free. Two of them lifted the young man aboard to a place on the furs by Virginia Albret's side. At once the crowd pressed forward, filling up the empty spaces.

Now Achille Picard bent his shoulders to lift into free water the stem of the canoe from its touch on the bank. It floated, caught gently by the back wash of the stronger off-shore current.

"Good-by, dear," called Mrs. Cockburn. "Remember us!"

She pressed the Doctor's arm closer to her side. The Doctor waved his hand, not trusting his masculine self-control to speak. McDonald, too, stood glum and dour, clasping his wrist behind his back. Richardson was openly affected. For in Virginia's person they saw sailing away from their bleak Northern lives the figure of youth, and they knew that henceforth life must be even drearier.

"Som' tam' yo' com' back sing heem de res' of dat song!" shouted Louis Placide to his late captive. "I lak' hear heem!"

But Galen Albret said nothing, made no sign. Silently and steadily, run up by some invisible hand, the blood-red banner of the Company fluttered to the mast-head. Before it, alone, bulked huge against the sky, dominating the people in the symbolism of his position there as he did in the realities of every-day life, the Factor stood, his hands behind his back. Virginia rose to her feet and stretched her arms out to the solitary figure.

"Good-by! good-by!" she cried.

A renewed tempest of cheers and shouts of adieu broke from those ashore. The paddles dipped once, twice, thrice, and paused. With one accord those on shore and those in the canoe raised their caps and said, "Que Dieu vous benisse." A moment's silence followed, during which the current of the mighty river bore the light craft a few yards down stream. Then from the ten *voyageurs* arose a great shout.

"Abítibi! Abítibi!"

Their paddles struck in unison. The water swirled in white, circular eddies. Instantly the canoe caught its momentum and began to slip along against the sluggish current. Achille Picard raised a high tenor voice, fixing the air,

> *"En roulant ma boule roulante,*
> *En roulant ma boule."*

And the *voyageurs* swung into the quaint ballad of the fairy ducks and the naughty prince with his magic gun.

> *"Derrièr' chez-nous y-a-t-un 'ètang,*
> *En roulant ma boule."*

The girl sank back, dabbing uncertainly at her eyes. "I shall never see them again," she explained, wistfully.

The canoe had now caught its speed. Conjuror's House was dropping astern. The rhythm of the song quickened as the singers told of how the king's son had aimed at the black duck but killed the white.

> *"Ah fils du roi, tu es mèchant,*
> *En roulant ma boule,*
> *Toutes les plumes s'en vont au vent,*
> *Rouli roulant, ma boule roulant."*

"Way wik! way wik!" commanded Me-en-gan, sharply, from the bow.

The men quickened their stroke and shot diagonally across the current of an eddy.

"Ni-shi-shin," said Me-en-gan.

They fell back to the old stroke, rolling out their full-throated measure.

> *"Toutes les plumes s'en vont au vent,*
> *En roulant ma boule,*
> *Trois dames s'en vont les ramassant,*
> *Rouli roulant, ma boule roulant."*

The canoe was now in the smooth rush of the first stretch of swifter water. The men bent to their work with stiffened elbows. Achille Picard flashed his white teeth back at the passengers,

"Ah, mademoiselle, eet is wan long way," he panted. "C'est

une longue traverse!"

The term was evidently descriptive, but the two smiled significantly at each other.

"So you do take *la Longue Traverse*, after all!" marvelled Virginia.

Ned Trent clasped her hand.

"We take it together," he replied.

Into the distance faded the Post. The canoe rounded a bend. It was gone. Ahead of them lay their long journey.

THE END

www.ingramcontent.com/pod-product-compliance
Lightning Source LLC
Chambersburg PA
CBHW030537180626
46810CB00005B/1904